Chasing the Jaguar

MICHELE DOMÍNGUEZ GREENE

Chasing the Jaguar

HARPER TEEN

An Imprint of HarperCollins*Publishers*

HarperTeen is an imprint of HarperCollins Publishers.

Excerpts from the song "Mariposa Traicionera"
appear on pages 104 and 221.

www.harperteen.com

Library of Congress Cataloging-in-Publication Data
Greene, Michele Domínguez.
     Chasing the Jaguar / Michele Domínguez Greene.—1st ed.
         p.   cm.
     Summary: After having unsettling dreams about the kidnapped daughter
of her mother's employer, fifteen-year-old Martika learns that she is a
descendant of a long line of curanderas—Mayan medicine women with
special powers. Includes glossary of Spanish words.
     ISBN 978-0-06-076355-8
     [1. Mayas—Fiction.   2. Indians of Central America—Fiction.   3. Self-
realization—Fiction.   4. Kidnapping—Fiction.   5. Quinceañera (Social
custom)—Fiction.   6. Los Angeles (Calif.)—Fiction.   7. Mystery and
detective stories.]   I. Title.
PZ7.G84243Cha 2006   2005022735
[Fic]—dc22   CIP
                                                                        AC

Typography by Sasha Illingworth
❖
First HarperTeen paperback edition, 2008

For my mother, Dorita

Acknowledgments

I'd like to thank the many people who helped me with this project: my agent, Victoria Sanders, for her belief in me and in the story; my manager, Marilyn R. Atlas, for thinking big and opening the first door; at HarperCollins my wonderful editor, Phoebe Yeh, for her patience, great ideas, and encouragement, and Whitney Manger for all her help and support. Among the many books I used in my research of Maya life and ritual, the scholarship of Robert Sharer (University of Pennsylvania), the late Linda Schele (University of Texas), and David Freidel (Southern Methodist University) proved invaluable. Ciro Hurtado, Luis Pérez, Jorge Mijangos, and Xavier Quijas Yxayotl were extremely generous with their knowledge of traditional musical instruments and drums of the Maya. Gordon Brotherston of Stanford University made a vital and important contribution with his expertise in Maya languages of the late pre-classic period. Doña Inez Navarro shared her vast experience as a *curandera* with me, for which I will be forever grateful.

I would also like to thank my family: my mother, Dorita; brother, Roland; and sister-in-law, Marisa. To my extended family of friends and colleagues who supported this project from the beginning, Hanna Weg, David Jensen, Dana DiCiano, Robert Katz, Adele Sylvester, Dwight Yoakam, and Heather Bridger-Ulloa, among many others, *gracias de todo corazón*.

Author's Note

The ancient Maya were a highly advanced civilization on par with the ancient Egyptians. They were thriving long before the arrival of the Spanish conquistadors. The Maya built amazing architectural cities; practiced medicine and astronomy; and had an organized, productive, and complex social and religious culture. As the Spaniards moved across the Yucatán peninsula, the Maya retreated deeper and deeper into the jungle to escape persecution. To this day, many modern Maya show no signs of the racial mixing, or *mestizaje*, that produced the Mexicans and other *mestizos* across Latin America. The traditional Maya healers and diviners, the *curanderas/os*, continue to practice today all over Latin America and in other countries that have a significant immigrant population.

In writing this story, I have woven together mystical practices from different shamanic cultures with the ways of the ancient Maya. There are basic similarities among such cultures pertaining to dream interpretation, telepathy, astral projection, and so on. While the references to history, social practices, and Maya deities and beliefs have been drawn from scholarly works, many of the true secrets of the Maya *curanderas* can be revealed only to the initiated, to those born with the power and called into the circle of Maya *curanderísmo*. I urge young readers to further explore the ancient Maya and their amazing history and perhaps one day take a trip to visit the spectacular ruins of Uxmal, Tulum, and the other archeological sites mentioned in this book.

The translations of Spanish words and phrases have been included on pages 221–227.

Chasing the Jaguar

One

❀

*M*artika tossed fitfully in her sleep, the same dream playing out again:

> She's lost, on a crowded, unfamiliar street . . . so many people, jostling and bumping her . . . passive, inscrutable Indian faces. Dense trees hover at the edges of the dirt streets, their canopy reaching, arching, as if trying to reclaim what was once wild. Somewhere in the green jungle a big cat lets out a screeching cry, and Martika knows it is for her. Something is following her, something is waiting for her, something powerful, foreboding. . . . What is it? Where is it?

The loud honking of the MTA bus on the street below her window jarred her awake. Martika broke out in a faint sheen of sweat. Outside the morning traffic was already getting out of control; frustrated drivers honked and lined up for the freeway on-ramp. Martika got out of bed and tried to shake off the dream.

Just a run-of-the-mill anxiety dream, probably related to finals, she told herself, making her way down the narrow hallway to the bathroom. In the past few weeks, her dreams had become strange and unsettling. Too many mornings she awoke feeling exhausted, as if she had been traveling a great distance. Powerful images of places she had never been lingered in her mind all day.

She turned on the water in the shower, stuck her hand in, and waited. Good, the Mendez family next door hadn't yet used all the hot water in the building. From the kitchen, the smell of *chorizo con huevos* filled the apartment, and she could hear her mother, Aurelia, listening to her favorite morning radio show, *El Cucuy de la Mañana.*

"Dime, mi amor, ¿crees que tu esposo anda con otra?" The annoying host was asking a caller about her marriage.

In a timid voice the woman answered, *"Pues creo que sí porque no regresó anoche hasta las tres de la mañana."*

Great, thought Martika, *that's all Mom needs to be listening to, complaints about a cheating husband.*

That was too often the topic in her family these days, since her father had moved out. As if on cue, she heard Aurelia bang a pot loudly and then shout, "Martika, hurry up! You're going to miss the bus!"

Martika slid out of her cotton pajamas and stepped into the

shower. As she squeezed the shampoo into her hair, the water turned cold. *Damn the Mendez family and their six kids.*

"We're going to pick up your dress today after school, okay?" Aurelia declared, heaping more *chorizo* onto Martika's plate. Martika nodded and put the last piece of tortilla into her mouth. She had changed the radio to a *rock en español* station, and Maná's hit "Mariposa Traicionera" filled the small kitchen. Her mother had a checklist for Martika's *quinceañera* in front of her.

"Then we pick up the party favors at Maria's and then we confirm the cake."

"Mom, we confirmed the cake last week."

"You can't be too careful. I had a cousin, Lupita, who ended up with a sympathy cake for her *quinceañera*. The bakery got confused and thought it was for a *velorio*. Poor thing, it actually had black frosting!"

Martika tried to swallow a laugh with her orange juice until she saw the sly smile on her mother's face as she continued, "It was dreadful. I laughed so hard I thought I would pass out, but Lupita didn't think it was funny. Your party is in two days; we're not having anything go wrong! And be sure to tell your father to double-check with that mariachi he hired, so they show up on time." She went back to the kitchen to scour the skillet.

Turning fifteen was an important milestone in Mexican

culture, marking a girl's entry into womanhood. Martika's parents took it very seriously. The guests, the party, the music—everything had to be just right. To top it off, the elaborate white dress made it seem like a wedding. It was planned for the coming Sunday since both her parents worked on Saturday and her school was having an administrative holiday on Monday. And they could attend the Sunday mass first, as was customary before the party. For now, her parents were making her crazy over the details of the *quinceañera*; just the night before, her father had called four times.

As far as Martika was concerned, the party caused more tension than anything else, especially with her parents separated and the family up in arms about it. The fact that her father, Camiso, had a new girlfriend only complicated matters. She didn't want to disappoint her parents or seem unappreciative, but the whole thing seemed silly, the idea of all those people watching her, everyone celebrating that she was finally a woman.

From her perspective, there was not much difference between being fourteen and fifteen, except that now she was having weird dreams and waking up exhausted every day. She rubbed her eyes and pushed the plate away just as her mother returned with warm tortillas from the stove.

"That's okay, Mom. I don't need any more."

"You only had two tortillas! I don't want to hear any of this no-carb nonsense, this dieting. I read about it at Mrs. Weg's house."

"I'm just not hungry anymore. I had two servings of *chorizo!*"

"Well, you could gain a few pounds. It's not good to be too skinny, like those white girls who starve themselves. I read about that when the car was being fixed last week."

Her mother read everything and subsequently worried about everything. If it wasn't the disease of the week, it was pollutants in the environment or gang violence or genetically engineered fruit. Martika often wondered if maybe anxiety was what kept Aurelia going through the day, what with cleaning houses across the city and then taking care of their own apartment with all the cooking and shopping and such.

"How'd you sleep last night?" her mother asked off-handedly.

Martika knew her mom was concerned about the strange dreams and trying to sound casual.

"So-so," she replied.

"No more dreams?"

"Yeah, but nothing out of the ordinary," Martika lied. She didn't want her mother obsessing about it all day. "Are you going to meet me at school?"

"I'll be there by three thirty," Aurelia replied. "I have a new half-day client over in Laurel Canyon."

"Well, if they look crazy don't go in," Martika cautioned her. Some of her mother's worrying was rubbing off.

"Oh no, they're okay. It's Mrs. Weg's son. He and his wife

both work, and they have no time to clean."

With a kiss, her mother stuck an extra banana in Martika's backpack. "And stay away from those gangbangers in the park."

Martika gave her a hug, then headed into the hallway and down the narrow stairway to the street.

A light mist hung over the Echo Park Lake, the giant palm trees swaying slightly as they reached high into the clear Los Angeles sky. There had been a strong wind the night before; it had blown out the thick layer of gray-brown smog that usually hung over the city. There were a few joggers circling the lake, a young mother with a baby stroller, an elderly man feeding the pigeons. Next to the park, the 101 Freeway snaked along, clogged with cars in both directions heading east to downtown or west toward the ocean.

At the drinking fountain, Martika's best friend, Lola Lopez, waited in her usual spot, her makeup perfect, her hair in an elaborate style with the top clipped up high and a ton of little braids cascading down. Martika marveled at it, impressed.

"Nice hair! It must have taken forever to do!"

Lola beamed, her full, glossy lips revealing a set of even, white teeth. "Thanks! It's all my own and I did the braids last night and then slept in a net, without moving."

"Lucky you. I woke up with the sheets tangled around me like a vine."

"More of those funky dreams with the *indios* and the jungle?"

Martika nodded. Her backpack felt heavier than usual today.

"Girl, you've got to take some Sominex or *yerbabuena* or something. You can't be dragging like this, especially with a big party this weekend. You want me to do your hair for it?"

Martika shook her head with a laugh. "You'll make me look like someone I don't recognize!"

"Your style is just fine, very natural and homegirl next door, but I could turn you into J.Lo!"

"And that's a good thing?" Martika retorted with a smile.

Martika's fashion sense was an ongoing topic of discussion between them. Unlike Lola, Martika did not consider herself glamorous: petite, still slim, and girlish with her long black hair pulled into a no-nonsense ponytail. She had her own style, made up of jeans and hip retro clothes she found trolling the resale shops on Sunset. Lola called it "tomboy vintage." Martika thought she looked like any of the girls in her neighborhood, but Lola always pointed out the one feature that drew attention and curiosity: her eyes. Her dark hair and olive skin were set off by a pair of oddly pale amber-colored eyes, circled by a dark ring around the iris. Lola said they looked like *café con leche*, with little flecks of iridescent gold in them. In a certain light they made her look like a cat. No one in the family had eyes like hers. She had long ago stopped asking her parents about them; no one ever gave her an explanation that made sense.

Martika and Lola started across the park, toward the bus stop. As they passed a group of guys dressed in gang colors, one of them called out to Lola. "*¡Hola, mujersota!* What're you doing later?"

The others snickered as Lola shot them a bored glance and kept on walking. She was used to the boys and men in the neighborhood flirting with her. She had always been a beauty—and now, at fifteen, she had a body that wouldn't quit, Latin style, with voluptuous curves and a round butt. But she wouldn't have anything to do with the neighborhood homies, especially since her middle brother, Javier, had taken to hanging out with them.

"What time will you be home?" Lola asked as they neared the bus stop.

"My mom's picking me up right after school, and we're getting the dress and the party favors. And checking on the cake. You know my mom told me she had a cousin that got a sympathy cake for her *quinceañera.*"

"Mine too!"

They laughed in unison and exchanged a high five. "Urban Mexican legend!"

A slight wind picked up and Martika felt a tingling at the base of her skull. Something familiar was at the edge of her mind, rustling, like many voices whispering. Or was it the wind in the palm trees? She rubbed her neck and closed her eyes. Lola's elbow jabbed into her ribs.

"Look, there's the witch! How long do you think until the car arrives?" Lola asked.

A slight elderly woman strode purposefully across the park. She moved fearlessly through the gangbangers and the sleeping homeless people. She lived in the big gray house perched on the hill overlooking the east side of the lake. She had lived there as long as anyone could remember. Tía Tellín was not afraid of anyone. The people around the park talked. They said that Tía Tellín was a *bruja*, a *curandera*, a shape-shifter; they said that she had the power. People were afraid of her; she could put the evil eye on you. But they went to her for advice also. They told her their fears and worries about relatives back home and asked for help getting a wayward boyfriend back. They called her *"tía"* or "aunt" as a sign of respect, and no one bothered her.

The girls watched as she arrived and waited at the corner. Her face was impassive; she did not make eye contact with anyone.

"Okay, one, two, three . . ." Lola started counting. By the time she got to nine, a dark sedan had pulled up and spirited Tía Tellín away.

"It's like clockwork!" Martika said. "Where do you think she goes? It's been going on for weeks now!"

"My mom says she must go to some secret meeting, some

society of *brujas* or something."

"I don't believe in all that, do you? That stuff about spirits and medicine men and all?" Martika asked.

Lola dropped her voice low. "My mom goes to a *curandera* and gets her cards read by a psychic in Eagle Rock."

"That's crazy!" snorted Martika. "This is Los Angeles. We're not living in some backward village!"

The MTA bus pulled up, crowded with students making their way to the local high school, Elysian. Lola waved to a group of girls from her history class. When the Elysian students got off the bus, it was still crowded. Martika had a thirty-five-minute ride ahead of her to the Los Feliz Magnet School for gifted students. She'd have to stand the whole way. She turned to Lola. "What're you doing after school?"

"I'm going to Pepa's house to practice on her hair for your party. My folks will probably be working late. Call me?"

"Sure, I think we're having *sopa de fideos* tonight if you want to come by to eat," said Martika.

"*¡Excelente!*" shouted Lola with a wave as she joined her friends.

Martika climbed aboard the bus. The exhaust came in through the windows as it pulled away, making her choke and cover her nose. She had a dull headache from not sleeping well. As the bus headed north to cross Silverlake, she looked up at Tía Tellín's gray house on the hill. It triggered a vague memory of something she couldn't pin down. Had the house been in one of her dreams, perhaps? She kept staring at it until it was hidden by the tall trees. The bus edged its way through the traffic, up the hills toward Los Feliz.

"Okay! Take your seats and when I pass by, and pick a slip of paper out of this jar!" said Ms. Osser, adjusting her rhinestone cat-eye glasses. Several boys wrestled, knocking into a girl named Hanna who hissed at them as she reached down to protect a tender new tattoo on her ankle.

"If you don't settle down, your punishment will be listening to the entire works of Andrew Lloyd Webber, in chronological order!" Ms. Osser shouted, waving her arms to make her point.

The students looked at her blankly.

"Isn't he the guy who wrote *Cats*?" asked Hanna, pushing back her dreadlocks.

"Yeah, my mom loves that old corny stuff!" moaned Damian, settling in next to Martika, a bag of greasy chips balanced on his notebook. "Please, anything but that!"

Ms. Osser moved down the aisles among her multimedia/art students. With her mop of curly magenta-black hair and a wife-beater T-shirt, she looked more like one of their peers than the teacher.

"Now, this jar contains slips with animal names on them. Whichever one you choose will be the subject of your final."

"Can't I just use my cat, Warlock?" wisecracked Damian.

He always tried to be the center of attention.

Ms. Osser ignored him.

"In many cultures, animals have great spiritual and mythological significance. You are going to research your animal and make an artistic representation of it. And I want you to use your imagination. Don't bring in a cutout from a magazine or a computer scan. Make it impressionistic," she said.

"Can we make a short film?" asked Damian, grabbing a handful of chips from under his desk. His father was a successful movie director, and Damian always tried to find a way to mention it to the class. "'Cause I'm sure my dad would let me use his editing bay and—"

Ms. Osser cut him off.

"Not this time, Damian—you've already made a short film this year. Try something different. And toss the chips. No eating in class."

Martika smiled. Ms. Osser didn't put up with jerks, nor did she suck up to the kids with well-connected parents the way some of the teachers did. Los Feliz Magnet had students from all over the city. It specialized in art and science programs, and there was a waiting list to get in.

Ms. Osser stopped at Martika's desk with the jar and looked over the rims of her glasses.

"Make it a good one."

Martika reached in and felt the small scraps of paper, turning them over between her fingers. She secretly hoped she'd get the horse. Then she'd have an excuse to visit the Arroyo Stables in Pasadena. Maybe she'd even have a chance to ride. She shut her eyes; two pieces remained in her palm. As her hand closed around one of them, it slipped through her fingers, like a silver-fish. She pulled the other one out. It read THE JAGUAR. The jaguar? Martika was disappointed; she knew it was a big cat but she wasn't even sure whether it had stripes or spots.

She didn't know that she hadn't chosen the jaguar at all. It had chosen her.

Two

❀

Saturday came, and Martika had a plan to get out of the house and away from the *quinceañera* madness. She and Lola would take the bus to the Los Feliz library, where she could check out research books. After a visit to the pet store across the street to look at the puppies, they would stroll down to Vermont Avenue and browse the used bookstore and funky shops, maybe get a bite at the House of Pies. On the way back, a stop at Uncle Jer's, which Lola considered the hippest boutique in town, although neither of them could afford anything there. While Martika lay in bed fine-tuning her plan she heard her mother talking on the phone.

"And how many margaritas did you have?" Aurelia asked angrily. Martika climbed out of bed and listened at the door.

"You know I need your help today, Mona! I have that huge house to clean for a party and I can't do it on my own. Mr.

Colton wants it spotless."

Mona was her mother's best friend. Sometimes she helped Aurelia if she had an extra-big job.

Aurelia's voice began to rise. "You know what I'm going to have to do? I'm going to have to ask Martika, when she has so much schoolwork to do. Does that seem right to you?"

Aurelia tapped on Martika's door and pushed it open to find her listening.

"Honey? I have to ask you a favor. *La Mona esa* had too many drinks last night at a party with Martín, and now she's in bed with a big *crudo*. Do you think you could help me with the Colton house today?"

Martika knew her mom hated asking for her help, and she didn't like to have her daughter cleaning houses. So she hid her own disappointment at losing her day out in the city and said, "Sure, if we can stop at the library later. I have to get some books for school."

"Of course."

Aurelia turned back to the phone. "Did you hear that, Mona? My sainted daughter is going to do the job, the day before her *quinceañera. Y tú tienes la culpa, ¡mujer desenfrenada!*"

Aurelia hung up the phone. Martika just smiled. Her mom could be so dramatic.

They pulled the beat-up Toyota Tercel onto Sunset Boulevard and started the long trek to the Pacific Palisades, where Ted

Colton lived. The freeway would have been faster, but Aurelia was too afraid to drive on it. Ted had been Aurelia's client for many years. He owned car dealerships all over the city, selling expensive cars: BMW, Porsche, Mercedes-Benz. Ted was extremely wealthy and enjoyed a flashy lifestyle. He and his wife, Nancy, had split up last year, and he had custody of their sixteen-year-old daughter, Jennifer.

"La madre se dio al trago." Aurelia had told Martika in a low tone that the mother had a drinking problem.

They drove through the city, passing barrios with mom and pop markets, Latin dance clubs, and specialty *carnicerías* and then into Silverlake, full of artsy, bohemian shops right up against the working-class storefront churches of recent immigrants from Central America and Mexico. There were trendy restaurants and crowded twenty-five-cent Laundromats all on the same block. Martika liked to come on the bus with Lola to buy vintage clothes at Ragg Mop or Retro Mania and just watch all the crazy, colorful people hanging out at the cafés and coffeehouses, reading *LA Weekly*.

Sunset cut across Los Angeles, past the El Chavo restaurant and the Tiki-Ti bar, past the Children's Hospital and into Hollywood. It wasn't the Hollywood of the movie studios and celebrities. It was the real Hollywood with a funky street scene and runaway teenagers from the Midwest trying to reinvent themselves.

They drove past Crescent Heights, and then they were on the Sunset Strip, where everything suddenly took an upscale turn, with the fancy nightclubs, the Chateau Marmont hotel, and huge billboards with images of the current supermodels splashed across them. At Doheny Drive the Strip gave way to Beverly Hills. Enormous mansions lined the wide, divided boulevard. Except for a few Latino gardeners who worked trimming, pruning, and raking leaves, the street was empty. Everyone seemed to live behind big gates with perfect green lawns and flower beds.

"Which one will you live in when you're a big, famous archeologist?" Aurelia asked her. This was a favorite game of theirs. They would choose among the fancy houses in Beverly Hills or Hancock Park. Martika waited; the one she liked best was a big Mediterranean with a high, whitewashed wall and bright red bougainvillea.

"That one!" She laughed, pointing as they passed it. "And what about yours, Mom?"

Aurelia pointed to a huge, plantation-style house on the other side of the street, a wide veranda wrapping all the way around it. "When I win the Pick Six, that's the one I'm buying!"

The Toyota made a hissing sound followed by a pop, and the engine started to lose power. Aurelia shifted to a lower gear.

"Don't worry," she said, "it's just getting overheated."

The Toyota chugged along, winding its way through the twists and turns of the boulevard.

About half an hour later they pulled up in front of Ted Colton's huge, Tudor-style house on Amalfi Drive in Pacific Palisades. Aurelia punched the special code to open the heavy, wooden gates. Ted's gleaming Mercedes-Benz was parked next to a baby blue Porsche Boxter convertible.

"Ted got that car for Jennifer on her last birthday," Aurelia explained when she saw Martika looking at it, wide-eyed.

Inside, the house was furnished expensively in modern, streamlined style. Ted's office was just off the foyer, and through the open door they could see him talking on the phone. He was in his late forties, good looking, his curly hair just starting to go gray. As he talked, he paced nervously, working a gold pen through his fingers. He nodded casually to Aurelia and Martika.

"How much can we get for it from the other guy? And can we do it today?" A pause, then, "Look, I don't want any trouble if we can avoid it, but I can't let a deal like this pass me by. I've got to go where the money is, you understand?"

Aurelia and Martika moved quietly to the utility closet for the feather duster, vacuum cleaner, and other cleaning supplies. Ted's loud voice carried out into the hallway.

"Don't worry about that—I can handle it with Blasi. I'll

move the merchandise. You just get the buyer in line," he said forcefully.

Ted hung up, dialed another number, and launched into another fast-paced conversation.

"J.T. is setting it up for today with the other buyer. It should all go smoothly and it'll be out of our hands by the end of the day."

Over the years Aurelia had told Martika that Ted had a lot of shady business dealings and questionable partners. Sometimes they came by the house in dark suits and sunglasses, quickly disappearing into Ted's office for a meeting. But it was none of Aurelia's business and she couldn't complain about Ted as an employer. He always paid cash, he gave her a nice bonus at Christmas, and he even paid to have her car fixed once.

When they moved on to the kitchen, Martika marveled at how clean everything was.

"Mr. Colton has business dinners almost every night," Aurelia told her, "and I guess his daughter is out with friends."

The refrigerator contained cases of bottled water, some bags of salad mix, and a couple of apples. *Cleaning this house is a piece of cake*, Martika thought. It was as if no one really lived in it.

"I'm going to finish down here for the party. Go clean up Jennifer's room, second door on the left at the top of the stairs." Aurelia turned back to polishing an ornate silver ice bucket, and Martika headed up the long, winding stairway. Jennifer was just a year older and Martika was curious to see her room. She opened the door and stood for a moment, taking it in. French doors opened onto a balcony that overlooked the large, lush yard and natural rock swimming pool.

There was a queen-size bed with an antique, handmade quilt, and on the desk sat a brand-new Mac Titanium Power Book. On the shelves she saw a top-of-the-line Nakamichi stereo, an iPod, a flat-screen TV, and a DVD player. Jennifer's room was immaculate; there was really nothing for Martika to do but dust. As she rubbed the lemon-scented furniture polish into the wood, Martika looked at the framed photos on the wall: pretty, blond Jennifer posing in her cheerleading outfit at school, raising pom-poms high in the air; standing at the Eiffel Tower with her dad; hiking up a volcano in Hawaii with her beautiful, stylish mother.

Being a teenager was about the only thing Martika seemed to have in common with Jennifer. She didn't want to feel envious but she couldn't help it. Why did this girl have everything? Martika was still saving for a computer so she wouldn't have to stay late after school or go to the library to use one. She peered into Jennifer's huge walk-in closet. Rows of trendy designer clothes hung neatly, color-coded to boot. On the wall racks, Jennifer had more shoes than Martika had owned in her whole life: sandals and boots, platforms and stiletto heels, sneakers by Nike and Skechers and Adidas. Martika thought of her mother, always making a point to stop by Payless Shoes when they were having a half-off sale, and how Ross Dress for Less was the only place they went for new school clothes.

In the corner of the closet something shiny caught Martika's eye, and she bent down to see a delicate bracelet with animal charms. It looked very old. It was made with yellow gold, and the animals' eyes were set with gemstones. It looked as if it had fallen off or been tossed aside. How could Jennifer have something so beautiful and treat it so carelessly? Martika decided at that moment that she didn't like Jennifer Colton. She reached for the bracelet to put it on the dresser when she heard giggling voices of teenage girls in the hallway.

"If I were you, I would've gotten an SUV, a big Escalade, or something that could hold a whole crew of people," one of the girls said.

Martika quickly slipped into the large bathroom that connected to a guest room. She waited on the other side of the door, listening. Thank heaven she'd made it out without being seen. Imagine being caught in the closet, checking out Jennifer's clothes! Through the door Martika heard the girls enter and flop on the bed. She shifted so she could see them through the crack of the doorjamb.

"Jen, did you see the way that Cody Hoblit looked at you when we were leaving The Promenade?" asked a skinny girl in tight hip-huggers that sat dangerously low on her abdomen.

Jennifer shrugged casually as she unpacked a shopping bag.

"Steph, he's going out with Cassandra Goldstein. He's not available."

Stephanie snorted, and a tall blonde picked up the thread of gossip.

"They've been together for, like, six weeks. And he's already done it with her. He's ready to move on! Jen, you should go for it!"

"He's been with practically every girl in our class, Whitney. I don't want everyone else's boy toy."

Whitney looked at her in disbelief. "He's the captain of the water polo team at Brentwood, fool."

"Plus," added Stephanie, "you don't want a guy with no experience, do you? I'd take a broken-in boy toy over some geek virgin any day!"

Jennifer squirted a spray of perfume on her wrist, ignoring her.

"Do you like the smell of this one? It's called Dirt."

"That's disgusting," said Stephanie, reaching for the remote control. "Did you TiVo the Jessica Simpson show? Nick Lachey is such a babe."

"I knew that marriage wouldn't last! You know she called my dad to discuss the divorce," Whitney chimed in.

Martika slipped quietly out into the hallway and downstairs as the girls' laughter mingled with the sound of the TV.

By four o'clock the house was spotless. Aurelia ran the

vacuum over the thick Persian rugs. The caterers in their white jackets began to arrive.

"Martika! I forgot the pool house! Can you run out there and give it the once-over?" Aurelia asked.

"Sure."

Martika walked through the breakfast room and out the sliding plantation doors to the yard. The pool house was bigger than their entire apartment. Inside it was clean but messy, with piles of new towels, inflatable chaise lounges, and inner tubes strewn across the floor. Martika began to stack them in a corner when she uncovered a beat-up cardboard box tied with a ragged string. It gave off an earthy smell. She felt the tingling at the base of her skull and a rustling sound in her ears. Or was it in her mind? She began to untie the string. The rustling sound grew louder. She heard the faint whispering of many voices speaking in an unfamiliar language. She reached into the box and felt something hard: a figure, wrapped in torn, faded newsprint. As she unwrapped it she heard Ted's voice approaching.

"You can take it over now—it's all arranged. He has the cash. . . ."

Martika quickly tossed the pile of towels over the box and sprayed some Fabuloso onto a rag to wipe down the counters. A moment later, Ted and another man opened the door. Ted looked at her, surprised, and then said, "Don't worry about cleaning up. No one will be coming out here during the party.

You can go back to the main house."

He waited while she gathered the towels and cleaning supplies. She had to make an effort to avoid looking at the mysterious box.

She brushed past Ted and hurried across the lawn to join her mother.

As the sun set low over the Pacific, Eddie Blasi looked out from a penthouse window high above the streets of downtown. He held a glass of expensive, flame-colored scotch. Eddie was tall and rail thin with hair the color of straw. His eyes were pale and inscrutable as he stared at the people below, scurrying along the crowded streets.

Like so many little bugs, he thought, dismissing them. Around him, the room was filled with exotic carvings and sculptures. He smiled at the thought of his newest acquisition, how he would place it among his other talismans of power. His collection contained pieces from every great shamanic culture on earth, artifacts that held profound spiritual power, instilled with the faith of so many believers. It had taken many years to assemble it and had cost an obscene amount of money, a good portion of it in bribes to get around museums and archeological authorities along the way. *But it was worth it*, he thought. The air hung heavy and still.

A tall, muscular man entered. Blasi didn't turn from the

window. "Where is it?" he asked.

The large man crossed his hands behind his back, uneasy. "Colton says he doesn't have it anymore. There was a miscommunication. Another buyer got to it first."

Blasi set down his glass, his narrow lips curling into a tense smile. The pupils of his pale eyes seemed to flatten; he looked like a snake about to strike. His voice was barely above a whisper.

"Ted Colton seems to think he can play this foolish little game with me, Tavo. I thought he knew better, but I guess he has a thing or two to learn."

Tavo shifted his weight, keeping his eyes down. Blasi continued, "Call the team. Call Mojito. Tell them we have an engagement this evening. I believe Mr. Colton is having a soirée."

That night Martika had the same dream. She was in a small, dusty town, at the edge of a dense jungle, on a street teeming with people. In the air, the distinct smell of burning, of ash and smoke. People hurried along, as if they were trying to get home, to someplace safe before . . . what? As she walked, pale yellow and brilliant purple butterflies fluttered around her, their delicate wings brushing her skin. A small, dark Indian man in traditional dress held out a carved stone amulet to her. She walked past him and he followed her, speaking to her in a language she did not understand. She moved away and he became more insistent, finally calling after her, distressed, as she disappeared into the crowd. In the distance, the smell of fire.

Martika woke with a start, anxious. She knew she should have taken the amulet from the man. It was important somehow, but now it was too late.

The clock at her bedside read 3:05 A.M. Martika got out of bed and looked at her reflection in the mirror, illuminated by the street lamp outside. Why did she keep having these intense, unsettling dreams? What was the tingling she felt at the base of her skull, the strange things she felt and heard in her mind? She knew that a disease like schizophrenia sometimes did not show up until a person was in her teens. Maybe something like that was happening to her? Martika climbed back into bed and closed her eyes, determined to fall back asleep and dream about flying or meeting Orlando Bloom, something normal that everybody dreamed about.

Across town, Ted Colton lay sprawled in bed, a generous quantity of vodka soothing his brain into a deep sleep. Beside him was a half-dressed blond woman, her long hair obscuring her face. She was a party guest who had been drunk enough to be invited to stay over. The house had been filled with hundreds of guests, too many people to keep track of, a lot of unfamiliar faces. The more the merrier, as far as Ted was concerned, as long as the liquor kept flowing and everyone had a good time.

In her bedroom, Jennifer slept soundly, worn out from an evening of being shown off as Ted's trophy daughter. The clock read 3:05 A.M. No one heard someone expertly deactivate the security system and cut through a large pane of glass. No one heard someone creep upstairs to Jennifer's room. She was awakened by a pillowcase being shoved over her head. A hand clamped across her mouth, and she felt the sharp sting of a needle in her arm. She struggled as a burning sensation spread through her muscle. Strong arms restrained her and carried her into the hallway. Her head swam and she felt her limbs become liquid. The cool night air hit her skin through her thin nightgown. She was barely conscious when she was tossed into a waiting van and the door slammed shut. It disappeared down the elegant, winding streets of the Palisades, leaving not a trace.

Three

✿

"*A*nd now as our Savior has taught us, we are bold to say, 'Our Father, who art in heaven, hallowed be thy name. . . .'"

Father Ricardo and the congregation at Church of the Sacred Heart of Jesus recited the Lord's Prayer. Martika glanced around the cavernous church. Some of the church-goers spoke the prayer in Spanish, their eyes shut tight, hands clasped to their breast. The church was beautiful, with stained-glass panels and an alcove for the large, painted statue of the Virgin of Guadalupe, patron saint of Mexico and the Americas. At her feet, below her green, star-covered robe, Camiso and Aurelia had laid bouquets of roses, asking for blessings for their daughter on this special day. After the Sunday mass, the entire family would head to her aunt Hortensia's house to celebrate Martika's *quinceañera.*

Martika's white dress felt itchy in the May heat. Luckily

she had put her hair up in a twist, but now black tendrils were beginning to escape. Across the pews she saw Lola doing her best to look demure in a flowing sundress, her ample breasts straining against the thin fabric. They exchanged a smile as the priest droned on. Martika felt her mother's heeled pump tap her ankle, drawing her attention back to the altar. Although she tried to look stern, Martika could see a smile just below the surface of her mother's pious expression. Aurelia thought Father Ricardo was as dull as *pan blanco*, but he was a man of God, nonetheless, and deserved their attention and respect.

After the presentation of the oblations, Martika took communion, accompanied by her beaming parents. Aurelia wore a new dress and had gone to the beauty salon to get her hair done; Martika thought she looked beautiful. The wafer stuck uncomfortably to the roof of Martika's mouth. She closed her eyes, trying to concentrate on her prayer, but when she did, she remembered the images from her dream the night before. Disturbed, she pushed the memory from her mind and filed back to her pew, taking a seat beneath the stained-glass window depicting Saint Christopher crossing the river with the baby Jesus.

Norteña music wafted out of Tía Hortensia's house in North Hollywood. In the backyard, paper streamers hung from the trees, steaming plates of *carnitas* and *picadillo* were devoured by guests who worked up an appetite dancing to Los Tigres Del Norte. Martika's feet were killing her as she danced once again with her father and endured wet kisses from second cousins and aunts who wore too much White Diamonds perfume and very red lipstick. Her father's dark eyes were shining, a mixture of pride and more than a few Tecates. Her parents had behaved remarkably well for people in the middle of a marital separation. They even danced to "*Solamente Una Vez*" at her grandmother's urging without getting into an argument. Now Camiso twirled Martika around as the accordion played a solo.

"Having a good time?" he asked.

"It's a great party, Papi. Thank you."

"Only the best for *mi princesa!*" He smiled as he reached into his pocket and pulled out a small package wrapped in plain white tissue paper.

"I meant to give this to you earlier but I forgot. It's just something little, from Yucatán. Josefina picked it out."

He had recently returned from a five-day vacation with his new girlfriend, Josefina. As Martika tore at the wrapping, Camiso continued, "Well, she didn't really pick it. We were outside an old *mercado*, and this little Indian guy came up to us, and he kept saying 'For your daughter.' He followed us, and when I went in to get a *guayabera*, Josefina finally took it. She says they do that with all the *turistas!*"

Martika held the gift in her palm. It was a stone amulet on

a thin leather cord, exactly the same as the one she had dreamed about the night before. She felt her stomach tighten and looked at her father's happy face. This was not the time to tell him about her dream. As he fastened it around her neck, something caught her attention. It was Tía Tellín, her piercing eyes staring at Martika through the swirl of dancing guests.

Did her parents invite her? They never gossiped with the neighbors about Tía Tellín. In fact, they never mentioned her at all. It seemed strange that they would invite her to the *quinceañera*. The amulet lay cold against Martika's collarbone and she instinctively ran a finger over it, meeting Tía Tellín's gaze. Camiso spun her into a *quebradita*-style do-si-do. When Martika turned around to look for Tía Tellín, she had gone. Martika's head felt light. She had a faint hum in her ears. When the music ended, Camiso hugged her and went to get a cold beer.

Martika moved through the crowd, looking for Tía Tellín. She was not in the house or on the front porch. She was not in the patio or in the backyard. She had vanished completely. Martika found Lola by the dessert table, munching a sweet tamale.

"Did you see her?" Martika asked.

"Who?"

"Tía Tellín! She was standing over by the back door!"

"Are you nuts? Why would your parents invite her?"

"I don't know. But I saw her, I know it!"

Lola motioned to Aurelia, who was getting a refill on her margarita.

"Mrs. Gálvez, you should get Martika some water or something. She's seeing things!"

"You don't feel well? Do you need to lie down?" her mother asked.

Martika jabbed Lola in the ribs. Lola grinned and went to join her older brother, Ramón, on the dance floor.

"I thought I saw someone . . ." Martika explained. Before she could finish, Camiso came over with Uncle Chuy, who wanted to take a family photo.

"Martika in the middle!" Camiso said, corralling them into position while Chuy struggled with his new digital camera. Aurelia noticed the amulet and asked, "Where did you get that?"

Martika didn't want to mention the sore subject of her father's trip to Yucatán, much less Josefina. She said only, "From Papi."

Aurelia leaned in and looked at it closely. Martika saw it was useless to think her mother wouldn't know where it came from; she was way too sharp for that. Aurelia's eyes got a hard, flinty quality to them.

"*Parece indio*, Camiso. Does it come from the jungle?"

Camiso cleared his throat, uncomfortable, keeping his eyes on Chuy.

"Yes. I got it in Yucatán."

Aurelia made a low sound in her throat and moved her arm to Martika's waist so that she could avoid touching Camiso's shoulder. The tension was thick and obvious. In an effort to change the subject, Martika asked, "Did you invite Tía Tellín? I could swear I saw her across the yard."

She felt her father's arm flinch and Aurelia's face lost its color for a brief moment. "You saw her? She was here? Did she try to—" asked Aurelia.

Camiso's voice was clipped when he cut her off. "Of course we didn't invite her. We don't even know her. Take the picture, Chuy."

His tone made it clear that the topic was closed. It seemed as if everything had gone from bad to worse in a brief moment. The camera flashed, blinding the three of them, and when her eyes had adjusted, Martika saw her father making his way into the crowd of guests. Her mother gave her an awkward smile and said, "You're getting overheated with all that dancing. Sit down and I'll get you some *agua de sandía*."

Martika watched Aurelia walk across the patio and serve the chilled watermelon juice with unsteady hands. Tía Tellín had been there, staring at Martika as plain as day. Now the old woman had disappeared and Aurelia looked as if she had seen a ghost. Martika began to wonder if maybe she *was* seeing things. She took the *agua de sandía* silently from her mother. Something strange was going on.

❀　❀　❀

Far across the city, in a dilapidated building in the industrial section east of downtown, Jennifer was led up a dirty stairway, a blindfold tied across her eyes. This was the third time she had been moved since her abduction. The men who had taken her from her house had handed her off to some other men. She hadn't seen their faces yet, but she knew one was called Mojito. He seemed to be the boss, ordering the others around, making the decisions. Their footsteps echoed off the walls; the building was empty. A slight draft blew down a hallway that reeked of rancid food and urine. They steered her into a room and she heard Mojito say, "Blasi says to give her food and water and always keep her in your sight. This can be an easy swap—no harm comes to anyone if it all goes smoothly. Wouldn't that be nice, *güerita?*"

He ran his hands along Jennifer's silky blond hair and she recoiled. Mojito gave a steely, cold laugh.

"Touchy, huh? You're lucky Blasi is running this show, because if it was me, you'd be getting a different kind of treatment from me and my boys, *güerita!*"

Jennifer's heart pounded, but she knew better than to show how scared she was. She wouldn't give them the satisfaction. She heard his footsteps going down the hallway. *Who are these people and what do they want from me?*

Four

❀

It was late when Aurelia and Martika returned home. Martika carried her shoes, limping on sore feet. Once inside she turned to Aurelia. "Mom, can you unzip this for me? I have to take a shower after all that dancing."

"It's your day. Stay in there for half an hour if you feel like it!" Aurelia helped her out of the party dress, and Martika disappeared into the bathroom.

Aurelia stayed for a moment, staring at the closed bathroom door. *In a few years, Martika will be done with college and on her way to a real life*, she thought.

She dreamed big for her daughter. At Martika's age, Aurelia had hoped to attend the university in Guanajuato, but her family had been too poor to send her or to spare the money her young hands could earn. At eighteen she had married Camiso, and they'd made the arduous trek north, crossing the border under the cover of darkness. She had put her own dreams aside, and now all her hopes were on Martika. Aurelia looked at the crumpled white dress, so much like a bride's. She told herself that when Martika married, she'd have her own career, her own life. Martika wouldn't be dependent or obedient the way Aurelia's own parents had taught her to be. Where had it gotten her? Camiso took up with that young girl, Josefina, from the construction office. Now Aurelia was separated, probably heading for divorce, and starting over at thirty-six.

She folded the dress and set it on the laundry basket by the front door. The answering machine in the kitchen blinked with a series of messages. Aurelia let out an audible groan. "Not tonight," she said, walking toward her bedroom. "Whatever it is, it can wait until morning."

Half an hour later, Martika climbed into bed, her black hair still damp. She drifted off to sleep, images from the party colliding together. Faces overlapped, scenes shifted.

Suddenly her senses became acute, the air smelled dank and musty, with a sharp astringent scent . . . something familiar. She was in a run-down room with a torn mattress in the corner, a thin blanket thrown across it. Through the barred window, the night sky was visible, cool air creeping through the cracked pane. Cockroaches scurried across the dirty floor, and in the walls she heard rats running back and forth, scratching against the stained and broken plaster.

Now she recognized the smell: urine. There was a sense of fear, of foreboding, about this miserable place. She sat curled into herself, against the wall, her head buried. Even in her deep sleep, Martika knew this was no ordinary dream. She felt as if she were in another person's skin, seeing through someone else's eyes, feeling someone else's fear. She tried to tell herself it was only a dream, tried to wake herself up, but she could not. She struggled to open her eyes. Her breath became short, she broke out in a sweat—

With a sudden jerk she pushed her body against the wall, jamming her shoulder but now wide awake. Her heart beat wildly as her eyes adjusted to the familiar surroundings of her room. What was that awful place? Why had she been there? She felt the amulet, clammy and heavy around her neck. This dream had been much more threatening than the previous ones. She clicked on the bedside lamp and reached for one of her library books. She would study for Ms. Osser's class. She was too afraid to go back to sleep.

The next morning, Aurelia found Martika sitting up in bed, asleep with a textbook open on her lap. She put it away and shook Martika by the shoulder.

"Honey? Didn't you sleep last night?"

Martika opened her eyes slowly, her lids heavy.

"I couldn't sleep so I got some schoolwork done."

Aurelia looked at her skeptically. Later she'd find out what was at the bottom of this, but for now there was something else to deal with.

"Ted Colton called six or seven times yesterday. He needs us to go over to his house immediately."

Martika's brow tensed. What did Mr. Colton want? That now they would go and clean up after his big party? Did he think they had nothing else to do but wait on him and his spoiled daughter?

"I'm not going back over there, Mom, and neither should you. He can hire a cleaning crew. Imagine the mess those people made!"

"It's not to clean, honey. It's something else. He didn't say what, but his voice sounded strange. It has to do with his daughter. I told him we'd come over as soon as we could get there."

Martika let out a heavy sigh as her mother left the room. *This is just great*, she thought. A sleepless night of unsettling dreams, and now she had to spend her day off making a trek across town to deal with the problems of some rich, screwed-up family.

When they pulled up at Ted Colton's house, it was apparent that something was very wrong. Several cars were parked in the driveway, and outside the front door two men smoked and talked nervously on cell phones. In the house people were milling about and a heavy tension was in the air, a sense of expectation and uncertainty.

Ted came out of his study to meet Aurelia and Martika. He was unshaven, with dark circles under his bloodshot eyes. He looked as if he hadn't slept or changed clothes in the past two days. He ushered them in and closed the door.

"Someone has taken my daughter—she's been kidnapped."

Aurelia let out a gasp and took Martika's hand.

Ted continued, "It happened the night of the party, or in the early hours of the morning. I was here but I didn't hear anything. They were experts; they deactivated the alarm, knew exactly how the house was laid out."

"I'm so sorry, Mr. Colton. I can imagine what you must be going through," Aurelia said.

He reached for a glass of scotch on his desk and looked at Martika. "You must be about the same age as Jen, right?"

Martika nodded. His voice was unsteady, as if he would lose his composure at any moment. "I've talked to everyone who was at the house that day. When you were here, did you see anyone strange? Was there anything that caught your eye or struck you as being out of the ordinary?"

His eyes were desperate. Martika and her mother looked at each other, knowing there was nothing they could add to what he already knew.

"Nothing, Mr. Colton."

"What do the police say?" Aurelia asked.

"I haven't called them. I was warned not to."

"But you have to, Mr. Colton," Aurelia protested. "How else can you possibly find her? They know how to handle things like this."

Ted took a long swallow of scotch. "I have a lot of business interests that could get me in trouble with the authorities. And they would be no good in this case. Eddie Blasi and the people who have my daughter have made it clear what they want."

One of the men stuck his head in the door. "I've got DiCario on the line. He has no news to report."

Ted grabbed the phone receiver, agitated. "What did Hayes say? How could you not get through to him? You're a private investigator! Tell him I'll pay whatever he wants. I need it back here *now!*"

Martika could tell that the person on the other end of the line wasn't saying what Ted wanted to hear. He hung up, frustrated. After a moment Aurelia asked, "Have you eaten anything, Mr. Colton?"

Ted shook his head, "I haven't eaten since the party."

"We'll go make you something. You have to eat, to keep your strength up. Your daughter needs you," Aurelia said, rising.

She motioned to Martika to follow her into the hallway.

Martika was grateful for an excuse to get out of the study. Why hadn't Ted Colton called the police? How was he going to handle it on his own? She watched Aurelia as she scrambled some eggs and Monterey jack cheese. As if her mother could read her mind, Aurelia whispered, "You see? That's what happens when you're always living on the wrong side of the law. When you need help, you have nowhere to go. *Dios mio*, I hope the poor girl is all right." She crossed herself and opened a drawer.

"Martika, can you go get me some more kitchen towels from the linen closet upstairs? They must have used all of them at the party."

"Be right back."

Upstairs, towels in hand, Martika passed Jennifer's room. She knew she shouldn't go in but she couldn't resist. She silently cracked open the door and slipped inside. She looked around at all of Jennifer's expensive toys and gadgets. A heavy sadness came over her. All those things couldn't help Jennifer now. On the dresser she saw the gold charm bracelet, with the animal figures and gemstones. It looked so small and fragile.

Martika picked it up, planning to return it to the jewelry box, but as soon as she touched it, a series of jarring images exploded in her mind:

Jennifer, with a pillowcase over her head, being carried down the stairs and out into the night . . . blindfolded, walking up a dark stairway . . . seated in the same frightening room she had dreamed about. . . .

Martika dropped the bracelet as if it had burned her. She looked in the mirror; all the color had drained out of her face, and her hands were shaking. She had no idea what had just happened, but she was certain that something in her mind was wrong, terribly wrong. She hurried from the room, closing the door firmly behind her.

On her way downstairs Martika heard a car pull up outside. A door slammed and then she heard a distraught woman call out, "Ted? Is she here? Is she back yet?"

The front door opened and Jennifer's mother, Nancy, walked in. Martika recognized her from the photos in Jennifer's room. Her large blue eyes were red and swollen from crying, and her fingers shook as she pushed back her curly hair, hastily pulled into a ponytail. Despite her anxiety, she was still beautiful. Ted came out of his office, a look of dread on his face.

"Hello, Nancy. How was your flight?"

Nancy's voice rang out, a metallic screech. "How was my flight? My flight was a nightmare, six hours trapped in the air, wondering what has happened to my baby. How did they do it, Ted? Weren't you home?"

He cleared his throat, trying to remain calm in the face of her fury.

"Yes, I was—"

Nancy cut him off, her voice rising. "Then how in the hell did they get in here and take her? What kind of father are you?"

Ted fired back at her, angry. "A father who can stay sober long enough to qualify for custody, which is a lot more than you can do, Nancy!"

Nancy reached out and grabbed a Chinese vase on the entry table. She hurled it at Ted and it crashed against the door to his study, scattering broken shards across the floor. A piece nicked Ted's cheek and drew a thin line of blood.

"How dare you?" Nancy shouted at him, hysterical. "This place is like a fortress. If they got in here and took her, it was a professional job. What is it they want, Ted? Something that mysteriously fell off the back of a truck into your hands? Something you got on the black market? It's your fault—it's because of you, it's the way you live, the dirty business you're in! You're the one to blame for this!"

She collapsed, sobbing, onto the stairs. Ted hurried past her, toward his bedroom, muttering under his breath, "Crazy bitch . . ."

Martika stood in stunned silence at the scene she had just witnessed. She didn't envy Jennifer Colton now. Even when her own parents didn't get along, they never behaved so badly toward each other. Aurelia stood subdued in the doorway to the kitchen, a plate of scrambled eggs in her hand. Without a word she started up the stairs. Martika turned to Nancy, who was crying uncontrollably. Wanting to do something, to help in some way, Martika remembered the images she had seen in her mind of Jennifer. She knelt down next to Nancy and whispered, "She's okay, I just know it. She's okay."

Nancy's face crumbled anew. She reached out her arm and pulled Martika into an awkward embrace. Martika leaned against her, embarrassed. Nancy smelled of liquor mixed with salty tears.

"Oh God, I hope so," Nancy whispered.

Five

On the drive home, Martika was strangely quiet. Aurelia assumed it was the shock of Jennifer's abduction. After all, the girls were almost the same age.

"You're worried about Jennifer, aren't you?"

"Yes. But I'm also worried about me," Martika replied.

Aurelia reached out and smoothed her daughter's hair. "Don't worry, honey. Nothing like that will happen to you. Ted Colton is mixed up with all kinds of crazy people."

Martika cut her off. "I don't mean about that. I'm worried that there's something wrong with me, with my mind."

"What do you mean?" Aurelia asked.

"You know the dreams I've been having? They're getting worse. I sometimes feel like I'm trapped in them, in someone else's mind. And I get these strange sensations, this tingling at the base of my skull—it's like something is hovering just at the edge of my consciousness. Like a weird déjà vu."

Aurelia drove in silence for a moment then asked, "Do you have premonitions?"

"Not really, but I see these images in my head." Martika took a deep breath, relieved to finally be talking about it. "Back at Mr. Colton's house I went into Jennifer's room. I was just looking around, imagining how scared she must be. I picked up a bracelet that was on the dresser, and as soon as I touched it, I could see Jennifer in my mind. It wasn't my imagination; it was . . . real."

Aurelia swallowed and took a moment before asking, "What did you see?"

"I saw her being taken by someone, I saw her in a blindfold, in a room somewhere. I know it was real, Mom. It was as if it was happening right in front of me!" Martika's voice cracked and she struggled against the tears that she felt rising behind her eyes.

"There's something wrong with me, Mom. I know it. . . ," she whispered.

Aurelia looked at her daughter's tears and felt her heart lurch toward her. Her own fear mingled with Martika's. Because she knew what was happening.

When Aurelia began dating Camiso, she had heard the rumors about the powerful line of *curanderas* in his family, women who had the sixth sense. They could see the future, sense things that others could not. They were healers, diviners. They read thoughts, communicated with the spirits, and traveled through time. People called them *brujas* or witches, *nagualas*, shape-shifters. Her own mother had cautioned her about getting involved with such a family, but Aurelia had been young and in love.

Then Martika was born with those same amber catlike eyes that came with the inheritance. Those eyes foretold who would have the gift. She and Camiso were making a new life in Los Angeles. They didn't want their daughter to be weighed down by old superstitions and beliefs. They wanted Martika to be like any other modern American girl. And she was. But now she was having these strange dreams and visions. The gifts she was born with had surfaced.

Aurelia knew that Camiso would be angry with her for what she was about to do. But she didn't care. Let him be angry. She had to do what was right and fair by her daughter.

She looked at Martika wiping the tears away with the sleeve of her jean jacket. Aurelia took Martika's hand, keeping her eyes on the road ahead of them.

"There's nothing wrong with you, honey. But there is something I have to talk to you about. I think it has to do with the dreams and the other things you're feeling."

"What is it?" Martika asked, unable to hide her nervousness.

"Do you remember when you were little and you used to ask us about your eyes? Why they were such a strange color?"

"Yes, 'cause you and Dad don't have eyes like mine."

"There are other people in the family who have the same eyes as yours. You just haven't met any of them."

Martika thought of the many guests at her *quinceañera* and wondered how there could be any more relatives. Aurelia went on, haltingly.

"Back in Yucatán, where your papi is from, life is different. Things happen there that don't happen in other places."

"Yeah, like hurricanes. And they have all those big pyramids that the Maya built," said Martika.

"Not just hurricanes or the pyramids . . . but other things. There is mystery . . . and magic. There are people who can do things that other people cannot."

Aurelia struggled to find a way to explain what she knew would sound crazy to her daughter. Ahead of them, Sunset Boulevard rose and banked against the winding curves of the Westwood hills. She continued, "In the jungle, there are special people, with special gifts. They are called *curanderas*, medicine women, and they have psychic powers—"

"You don't believe all that, do you, Mom?" Martika asked, cutting her off.

Aurelia looked at her briefly, then said, "I didn't want to believe it. But I'm starting to. Martika, in your father's family, for many generations there has been a line of *curanderas*, women who can do incredible things."

Martika's heart beat rapidly and she asked, "But even if

they can, which I don't believe, what does all that have to do with me?"

"It is a legacy, a gift that is not passed down to every woman. Sometimes it skips generations at a time. But the next in line is always known by her eyes. The gift comes to those born with amber-colored eyes, like a cat."

Martika felt her stomach turn over. It sounded like something from a science-fiction story. But she also knew her mother was as practical and levelheaded as a person could be. After a beat she asked, "Do you think that has something to do with these crazy dreams and stuff?"

"I think it may. Papi's grandmother had the gift, and so did her sisters. But here in the U.S., your father and I didn't want you to be influenced by those old wives' tales. This is a different world, and we didn't want you pulled back into the one we left behind."

They drove in silence for a while. Martika tried to absorb everything her mother was telling her. A psychic legacy? Mind reading? How could any of that be real? Martika had never believed in things like that. She planned to be an archeologist, a scientist. She believed in the things that could be seen and proved. But there was no other way to explain what had happened in Jennifer's room with the bracelet. She knew in her gut that what she had seen was real.

The Toyota turned onto Echo Park Boulevard, but instead of going to the right, toward their apartment, Aurelia made a left and headed up the hill, east of the park.

"Where are we going, Mom?"

The car sputtered and lurched up the steep hill, stopping outside the wild, overgrown fence that surrounded Tía Tellín's house. Outside the gate a large jacaranda tree dropped its purple blossoms all over the street, leaving a carpet of brilliant color. Aurelia looked at Martika and said, "I cannot explain all of this to you very well. I don't even understand it myself. But there is someone who can. The time has come for you to know the truth."

Martika followed Aurelia out of the car. Aurelia pushed open the rusted iron gate to the garden and motioned for Martika to follow. On the porch Aurelia whispered, "Don't tell your father we came here, but Tía Tellín is your great-great-aunt on his side of the family. She understands all about this legacy or whatever it is."

As Aurelia knocked, Martika's mind raced. *Tía Tellín was her relative?* She remembered how her dad acted as if she didn't exist. How could it be that her great-great-aunt had lived so close to them all these years and she had never known? They heard light footsteps and then the heavy door creaked open. Inside stood Tía Tellín, her gray hair pulled back into a severe bun. She looked so small and fragile that it seemed as if she might blow away. In a quiet but firm voice she said, "You didn't know because your father didn't want you to know, *mija. Pero ya ha llegado la hora . . . pasen, están en su casa.*"

She invited them in. Martika tried to hide her unease. How had Tía Tellín read her thoughts? Tía Tellín showed them into the old-fashioned parlor, decorated with formal Victorian brocades and delicate lace curtains. Indian figures of people and animals stared at them from the bookshelves amid cracked leather-bound volumes. A jaguar carved from black obsidian sat on the top shelf. Aurelia shifted uncomfortably, not knowing where to look. Finally she settled next to Martika on a claw-foot sofa.

"Would you like some *yerbabuena* tea?" asked Tía Tellín.

"That would be very good, Señora. Gracias," said Aurelia stiffly. She was clearly intimidated by this tiny woman. Martika couldn't help staring at Tía Tellín's eyes: amber colored with a dark ring around the iris, which held iridescent flecks of light. Eyes like her own. Martika felt the faint tingling at the base of her skull. But now she was more curious than afraid.

Tía Tellín poured three cups of tea. Aurelia took hers, grateful to have something to do with her hands, something to focus her attention on. Tía Tellín sat back in a large wing-tip chair and asked, "How was the *quinceañera*?" Her manner was formal but there was something familiar about it as well.

"I thought I saw you there, in the crowd at Tía Hortensia's house," Martika answered.

Tía Tellín smiled enigmatically. "Oh no, *mija*, I was here at home. But you know what they say about *curanderas*. They can be in two places at once."

Aurelia's hand shook so much that she spilled her tea. As she bent to wipe it up, Martika leaned down to help, and her eye caught the statue of the jaguar. It seemed as if his gaze was following her. She thought about the research she had done for Ms. Osser's class. She knew that the jaguar was the revered spirit of the Maya but she hadn't gotten much further. Again Tía Tellín read her thoughts.

"It was no coincidence that you chose the jaguar for your class project, Martika. There are very few things that we can call coincidence. Everything is connected; every moment has a meaning even if it is not clear to us initially."

"How did you do that?" asked Martika. "How did you read my thoughts?"

"I'm sorry, that was rude of me. I'm an old woman and I forget sometimes."

"But *how* did you do it?"

"Telepathic communication is a skill that requires time and practice to develop, but it is a natural gift. It is simply more apparent and more powerful in some people than in others. Which brings us to what you are doing here today." She turned to Aurelia and asked, "Why now? After so many years of not wanting her to know?"

"Because she is having dreams—she's feeling things with her mind and she doesn't know what they are or what to do about them. I don't know how to explain it to her. And I know you do."

Tía Tellín took a long, slow sip of her tea. Aurelia clutched her steaming cup. Had she been presumptuous in bringing Martika? Maybe after so many years of silence, Tía Tellín didn't want anything to do with them. Maybe the whole thing was a mistake.

Tía Tellín set down her teacup. "Martika, it is never too late to begin the training of a *curandera*. If I'd had my way, I would have started teaching you many years ago, but your father didn't want that. Even when your family moved here to Echo Park and you lived just across the lake from me, I respected his wishes. He is your father, after all. But you mother did right in bringing you here today."

Relieved, Aurelia asked, "Can you explain to her what's going on?"

Tía Tellín's voice grew quiet, but somehow it seemed to drown out the sounds of the street and the freeway traffic.

"We are descendents of a great race, Martika. Our ancestors are the Maya of the Yucatán Peninsula, of Guatemala, of Honduras, and of Belize. They had a highly advanced civilization that included astronomers, artists, and shamans. Theirs was a world filled with magic, mysteries, and spirits. The most powerful and revered spirit was the Sun God, also known as the Jaguar, the shape-shifter. Each night, the Sun God descended to Xibalba, the underworld, and he became the Balam-Agab, the fearsome Jaguar God. After wrestling with the forces of death, he burst forth the next morning as the Sun

God once again, bringing new life."

Tía Tellín paused, took another sip of her tea and continued, "Many years ago, a woman in our family became the most powerful virgin priestess in the temple of Ixchel, the moon goddess. Her name was Xusita. She was your great-great-great-aunt many times removed, and she was mine also. In those times only men from the royal lineage were allowed to be priests in the temples. And sometimes to please the gods, a young virgin was sacrificed and thrown into one of the deep wells, the sacred *cenotes*. Xusita was just a girl of fourteen when this happened to her—"

Shocked, Martika blurted out, "Didn't she drown?"

"She should have. But three days later she emerged from the *cenote* with the teeth of the jaguar and tales of Xibalba. Her soul had merged with the Balam-Agab, and she was rewarded with great gifts. Gifts to travel through time, to move through the veil between the worlds of the living and the dead, to see the future in dreams."

"Could she also see the past in dreams? Because I had a dream like that . . . about this."

She reached into her T-shirt and pulled out the stone amulet. Tía Tellín leaned in and looked closely, running her bony fingers over it. She stared at it for a long time, and when she finally spoke, her tone was somber.

"It is one of the Itz flower stones of the Nunnery Quadrangle at Uxmal. How did you get this?"

Martika shifted uneasily. "From my dad. He said a vendor in Yucatán gave it to him, said it was for his daughter. Papi thought it was a gimmick for tourists."

Now Tía Tellín leaned back and smiled. She put her small hands together.

"Your father? And he is the one who wanted to keep you from knowing about your legacy? Why, he gave you one of the most powerful talismans of our people, and he didn't even know it! The Itz flower carving marks a place as magic; it adorns all the great places of power in Yucatán. You see? One can never change the course of destiny. The amulet is helping to draw the power to you. Tell me, *mija*, what is it you have been feeling?"

Martika looked to Aurelia, who gave her a slight nod of reassurance.

"It started with dreams in the past few weeks." She recounted the dreams of the jungle, the sense of foreboding, being surrounded by butterflies. Tía Tellín nodded and said, "The butterfly is transformation, it is freedom. It is you becoming who and what you are destined to be. That is normal. You were approaching fifteen, which is when the gift comes to life, full force. It was stirring your subconscious, calling out to you. You feel as if you traveled a great distance because you did. You traveled to the land of your ancestors, and who knows for certain which is real and which is the dream? Perhaps this thing we call reality is the true dream state. . . ."

Martika finished her sentence, "And the dream is the true reality?"

Tía Tellín's smile grew. "Exactly. Go on."

Martika continued, more confident now. "In the jungle there is always the smell of fire. I can't see the flames but I can feel fear in the air."

Tía Tellín flinched almost imperceptibly but said nothing. Martika continued, "Then I was on a crowded street and an Indian man called out to me. He offered me this amulet but I didn't take it and I knew I should have!"

"But it found you, didn't it?" asked Tía Tellín. "The universe unfolds exactly as it should, *mija*, even when we do not understand it."

"And then the dreams changed. . . ." She described the dirty room, the oppressive fear she felt, as if she were in someone else's mind. Tía Tellín's expression grew serious.

"Anything else?"

Martika told her about holding Jennifer's bracelet, about the clear images she saw in her head, how she knew they were real.

Outside the sun was setting. A faint purple light fell across the polished oak floor, casting odd shadows. Tía Tellín moved to an antique brass lamp and switched it on.

"What you experienced with the bracelet is called psychometry. You see images in your mind when you hold an object invested with the energy of the person it belongs to. And who is the girl with the bracelet?"

"She is the daughter of one of my clients," said Aurelia. "I'm the housekeeper for the family."

"And she is your age, Martika?"

"A year older, but I don't even know her. I just saw her once."

"You have a powerful link to this girl. There is no such thing as coincidence. You have a lot of work ahead of you."

"What kind of work?" Martika asked warily.

"You have to learn how to use your gifts, how to control and develop them, how to make them work for you. Right now they are running wild in your mind, and you have no control over them at all. That is why you thought you were going crazy. The gift is nothing to be afraid of. You can use your powers to do good, for the world and for others. But first, we have to decipher why the missing girl is reaching out to you."

"But what if I don't want to? I mean, what if I don't really believe in all that?"

Aurelia shot Martika a nervous glance. Tía Tellín smiled.

"You can turn away from the gift, but it will never turn away from you. The dreams will continue, the sensations, everything. You can try to ignore them or you can try to understand them. Your destiny will always find you, Martika, even when you want to escape it."

Martika was torn. She was curious and wanted to know more about this legacy and the history of her people. But the idea of psychic powers seemed unreal. How would she learn to use them? Would she seem different to her friends? Part of her wanted to run straight home and forget that this afternoon had happened. But she knew she couldn't go on with the strange and frightening dreams.

Your destiny will always find you.

She looked to Tía Tellín. "Are you going to teach me?" Martika asked, her voice a mixture of excitement and fear.

"You will come by regularly, after school. I will instruct you. There will be a lot of work and reading." She gestured to the ancient volumes on the shelves. "We will make up for lost time. Shall we begin tomorrow?"

Martika sat silent for a moment, considering, and then answered, "I'll come right after school."

Aurelia set down her tea, relieved. Now it seemed silly that she and Camiso had not brought the girl to Tía Tellín years before. She wasn't so frightening after all. Besides, what mattered most was that Martika was no longer afraid—that she had someone to help her, someone who understood what she was going through.

Tía Tellín waved good-bye and shut the heavy door, watching as Aurelia and Martika climbed into their car and descended the steep hill. Her face darkened. The things Martika described were gifts that took years to develop. Martika was experiencing them with no training at all.

The girl is powerful, she thought, *perhaps the most powerful of all our line. And it has fallen to me to train her, to guide her. So many questions to answer . . . the missing girl, the scent of fire, of burning . . .*

She felt a stirring in the stillness of the room.

Soraya . . .

Tía Tellín put the thought out of her mind and moved to the picture window. She was old; she could feel the strength of her younger days ebbing. She stared out across the park, the lake opaque and silent, the trees casting tall shadows. She hoped she was up to the work that lay before her.

Six

❋

Martika sat cross-legged with Lola at the edge of the Echo Park Lake. It was earlier than their usual meeting time. The wild parrots in the palm trees were beginning to squawk and screech; the freeway traffic was starting to build. Martika had just finished recounting the story of her incredible meeting with Tía Tellín. Lola twirled a long strand of black hair through her fingers. The rhinestones on her manicured nails reflected in the morning sun. After a moment's silence she asked, "So you're like a witch or something? Like Harry Potter?"

"Not magic or wands or any of that—"

Lola cut her off, holding back a laugh. "How do you know? Maybe you're going to learn to fly on some cool rig? Maybe a mop?"

"It's not a joke, Lola. It's real. Tía Tellín read my mind and she told me—"

Again Lola interrupted her. "I don't doubt that she read your mind. She's a *bruja*! Everyone knows that. But this stuff about *you* having special powers? I thought you don't believe in that."

"I didn't. And part of me still doesn't. But it's the only thing that makes sense with these crazy dreams and that episode with Jennifer's bracelet. I saw her as plain as I can see you right now."

Lola's expression soured. "That doesn't make any sense to me, Martika. I don't know how that could work."

"I don't know, either," Martika agreed. There were a lot of things she didn't know anymore. Like why Lola was making fun of her.

Down the boulevard, the MTA bus sounded its horn and Lola rose to her feet, smoothing her short black skirt.

"Come on, you're going to miss the bus." She gave Martika a hand up and they walked to the bus stop in silence. A large group of students got off the bus and moved past them.

"I guess it's kind of cool, you know? All that *curandera* stuff . . ." Lola trailed off. She didn't sound as if she really meant it; Martika didn't think Lola thought it was cool at all.

"Are you coming over for dinner?" she asked.

"Aren't we hooking up after school to go to Pepa's? She has the new Maná DVD," Lola said.

Martika winced. She had forgotten about the plans they made last week.

"I can't. I'm going to Tía Tellín's after school," she said apologetically.

Lola shrugged casually, but Martika could tell Lola was trying to act as if she didn't care.

"Cool. I'll call you from Pepa's, you know, about dinner."

Lola waved and hurried to join the group of other kids. Martika looked after her and felt a heaviness in her chest. Why did Lola have to be like that? She thought Lola would be as amazed as she was about everything with Tía Tellín. She took her seat on the bus and looked out the dirty, streaked window, trying to find Lola in the crush of students. The bus pulled away slowly from the curb.

Ted Colton poured another two fingers of scotch into his glass. It was only noon and he was on his third drink. It had been two days and the private investigator, Mike DiCario, had come up empty-handed on Jennifer. The only thing he had discovered about Jennifer's kidnapper, Eddie Blasi, was that he had a very long reach. He was involved in all kinds of illegal activities: drugs, stolen art, and smuggling. A loyal crew of thugs went everywhere with him, and he had connections to the powerful gangs that controlled street crime across large sections of the city.

Ted knew what Blasi wanted; he had underestimated how badly he wanted it. How could it be that valuable? Ted sat back in his leather chair, swiveling it on its base, side to side.

All of this for a chipped and broken relic that wasn't even one of his most expensive finds. Ted had moved a lot of stuff in the black market, stuff you could really get in trouble for. Who would ever have thought that old, beat-up jaguar statue would cause all these problems? That Blasi would kidnap his daughter over it? It had already been two days; he didn't want to imagine what Jennifer was going through. *If they lay one finger on her . . .*

He wouldn't let his mind go there. He closed his eyes; his head felt heavy and dull. The phone rang, cutting through the quiet room like the screech of a hyena. His hand fumbled for the receiver.

"Hello?"

After a beat of silence Eddie Blasi's voice came on the line.

"Hello, Ted."

"How's my daughter?"

Blasi ignored his query.

"Any progress?" Blasi's voice was steady, no inflection.

Ted cleared his throat. "I'm trying to get in touch with the other buyer—he's gone overseas. I'm sure I can get everything arranged as soon as I explain the situation to him."

He lied. He had already told the other buyer, R.J. Hayes, about Jennifer's kidnapping. And Hayes couldn't have cared less. He had left on a flight to Morocco and wouldn't be back until late summer, leaving the statue somewhere in his fortresslike estate in Malibu. Maybe.

"Good. Because I don't have a lot of patience," Blasi said. "Just so we all understand our time frame here, you have seven days to get me that jaguar. If not, you'll never see your daughter again. And won't that be a shame? The poor girl hasn't been feeling too well."

Ted felt his face flush hot with rage. "Is she sick? Have you done something to her?"

Blasi remained silent for an interminable moment. "She's fine. But scared to death. Seven days."

The line went dead.

A ratty pigeon perched against the bars of the window in the room where Jennifer was confined. They had removed the blindfold and untied her hands. Her wrists still burned where the rope had cut into them.

Her guard, a young man named Kiko, sat silently on a folding chair across from her. He had short-cropped hair and he wore a baggy pair of Dickies and a long white T-shirt. Under his sleeve, Jennifer could see several tattoos. He was obviously a gang member. Since they had brought her to the abandoned building, Mojito had put a string of sullen gangbangers in charge of watching her. To keep an eye on things, he dropped by several times a day. Whenever she heard his heavy footsteps on the stairway, her chest tightened. Mojito was unpredictable, always amped up on something, probably speed or cocaine.

She watched as a cockroach skittered across the dirty floor, heading toward her mattress. She tossed an empty soda cup at it.

"Do you know what time it is?" She turned to Kiko. He shrugged and gave an unintelligible answer.

Jennifer pressed on. "First period must be starting soon. I'm supposed to be in finals next week."

Kiko didn't look at her or respond. He pulled a rolled-up comic book from the pocket of his pants and began leafing through it. After a moment of silence, Jennifer asked, "What're you reading?"

Without looking up, Kiko replied quietly, "*Hellboy*."

"I liked the movie. Did you see it?"

Kiko shrugged again, uncomfortable. "It was okay."

Good, thought Jennifer, *now we're making some progress.*

In the days since her abduction, she had been planning. The previous year she had read a book on forensic psychiatry for her social sciences class. She had been fascinated by the criminal mind and had read as many books as she could find on the subject. She hadn't bothered to tell Whitney or her other friends on the cheerleading squad about it; they would've thought she was a freak. She remembered reading that the victim had to make her captors see her as a real person, with feelings. She had to connect with them in some way so that they wouldn't harm her. She turned again to Kiko.

"Did you see *Dawn of the Dead*, the new one?"

He shrugged, keeping his eyes on the comic book.

"Usually a sequel isn't as good as the first, but that wasn't true this time," she said. Kiko didn't respond.

"It was pretty cool. . . ." She trailed off, unable to keep the monologue going.

In the near-empty room, her voice sounded so small. She felt tears coming on and blinked to hold them back. Why was this happening? Why hadn't anyone come to help her? Did her father even know she was missing? She hardly saw him when he was home; he was always so busy. Sometimes she went days without having a real conversation with him. Maybe he thought she was at Whitney's or Stephanie's? Maybe he had no idea she was locked in this horrible place. Maybe no one was looking for her. The thought made her throat tighten, and her breath came out short and uneven. Kiko kept reading, unaware.

Outside, they heard the clunking of Mojito's army boots on the stairway. Kiko put away the comic. Mojito shoved the door open and stepped in, holding a bag of take-out food. It was stained with orange grease.

"*¡Hola, güerita! ¿Como estás?*" he asked. His voice had an unnerving singsong rhythm to it.

"Fine," Jennifer answered.

"I brought you some breakfast. Kiko, go keep watch with my boys outside."

Kiko left the room obediently. Jennifer felt her heart beat faster. She looked at the ground, afraid. Mojito stared at her, his eyes hard and shiny, his unruly black hair falling around his face. He was short and stocky, muscle bound from too many hours spent in the exercise yard. His thick neck merged solidly with his shoulders, and the intricate tattoos on his back showed through the thin cotton of his T-shirt.

He looks like an angry bull, Jennifer thought as he pushed a soggy plate of greasy enchiladas toward her. She didn't take the plastic spoon he offered.

"You not going to eat? You going to pull some of that pouty, rich-girl crap on me, *güera?*"

"I'm not hungry." The food looked disgusting.

"No? And what? You think I'm gonna come back later when you are? Or is it that you're not used to eating food like this? Maybe you want me to bring you some fancy restaurant food, some sushi or crap like that?"

His voice was rising; she could sense that he was getting agitated. She took the spoon and dug it into the enchiladas.

"That's a good girl." He reached out to touch her long blond hair. She pulled away from him. He sat back on his heels, grinning at her.

"You don't like me touching your hair, huh? Maybe you don't like having anyone touch you at all?"

His voice dropped to a low whisper. "Or maybe you do?"

She tried to hide her fear as he leaned in, his face inches from hers. She could smell his cologne, mixed with cigarettes and something else, something metallic and bitter on his breath.

"Maybe you'd like that a lot, huh? How about you and me, *güera* . . . getting a little action?"

Jennifer kept her eyes on the food but she couldn't focus. All she could see was a blur of orange cheese. Her hand was unsteady when she lifted it to her mouth. Mojito rocked back and forth, laughing.

"Scared you for a minute there, didn't I, *güera*?"

She swallowed a bite of the food and found the courage to ask, "Why am I here?"

"She talks! *¡Qué milagro!* You don't know, baby? You're here because your rich daddy screwed with the wrong guy in a business deal."

"What is it you want?"

"It ain't me, *güera*. I'm just taking orders from the top. Your daddy has to make it all right, and who knows when that will be? I hope it's not anytime soon."

He smiled at her. She shifted, uncomfortable.

"Does he even know what's happened?" she asked.

He laughed as he stood up. "Don't ask me. I'm just the capo, you know? I run these street boys but I'm not in charge of this show. I'll be back later."

He left. In the hallway, she heard him giving orders to Kiko and the others in Spanish. Jennifer looked around the room at the paper plate of greasy, coagulated food, the barred window, the dirty mattress. She had to get out of here.

Seven

✿

In study lab, Martika Googled "Mayan mythology" and came up with page after page of links and websites. She was determined to have some more information when she showed up at Tía Tellín's that afternoon.

She browsed the most promising sites and read about the Maya of Guatemala, of Yucatán, and of Honduras. She scanned the photos of the impressive palace at Tikal, the ocean front city of Tulúm and the great pyramids of Chichén Itzá. She scrolled through the information on the screen:

The Maya were the first to discover the concept of zero; they developed a calendar centuries before the Europeans that was accurate two thousand years into the future. Their architectural designs aligned with the orbit of the planets, showing a deep understanding of astronomy.

She clicked on the pantheon of Mayan gods, and a long,

detailed list of deities came up. What had Tía Tellín said about their ancestor? She had been a priestess of Ixchel. Martika typed in the name "Ixchel." A photograph of a stone carving of an old woman wearing a serpent coiled on her head and a skirt of crossbones appeared. Martika scanned other pages on Ixchel and saw Itz flower carvings that matched the amulet her father had given her. They decorated the shrine of Ixchel on Isla Mujeres, or Cozumel.

The Itz flower carving marks a place as magic. . . . Tía Tellín's words echoed in her head. Martika was so engrossed in the history of the Maya that she didn't notice when Ms. Osser walked up behind her desk.

"Ready for your finals?"

Martika looked up with a start.

"You look like you just saw a ghost!" Ms. Osser said with a laugh.

"I'm doing my research on the jaguar," Martika explained.

"So you're reading about the Maya, right? You should see the ruins of those pyramids. They are quite impressive."

"You've been to Yucatán?" Martika asked, surprised.

"I know it's hard to believe that your boring old teachers do anything besides show up here and assign a lot of homework. But sometimes we do interesting things. I even went there with a boyfriend!"

Martika laughed. Ms. Osser leaned in and clicked on the mouse to bring up another site. She pulled up an image of the great palace at Palenque in Guatemala.

"Look at that, Martika! The history of the Americas doesn't begin with Christopher Columbus or the Pilgrims landing at Plymouth Rock. It begins right there." Ms. Osser pointed to the impressive image on the computer screen.

"It begins with the Mayan kings."

Ms. Osser moved on to another student. Again Martika heard Tía Tellín's words.

We are descendants of a great race. . . . Martika felt an unfamiliar flush of emotion. Looking at the image of Palenque, she realized it was pride.

Martika's calves ached as she walked up the steep hill to Tía Tellín's house. She pushed open the front gate and found Tía Tellín waiting on the porch, holding a tall glass pitcher.

"Would you like some lemonade?" Tía asked.

"Lemonade would be great," Martika replied, following Tía Tellín into the house.

I hope it's not too sweet, Martika thought.

Before she could taste it, Tía Tellín said, "Don't worry. I only add the minimum of sugar; I like it natural."

She did it again!

After a swallow, Martika said, "I'm going to have to be careful what I think around here."

"That's actually a good place to start. You have to learn to think of your thoughts, the energy you put out, as a language all its own, as powerful as the spoken word, if not more so."

"How do I do that?"

"It's a change in your consciousness. It will come more naturally in time. For now, just imagine that your mind is a big movie screen and every thought can be read by other people."

Martika frowned. "I'd hate that."

"It will teach you to focus, to be aware of how you use your mind. Your thoughts are the blueprints for your life—they are what you manifest. And your dreams are something else altogether. They are the source of wisdom, of guidance. For the *curandera*, dreams are the first place of power. They are a portal to the otherworld, through the veil that separates the dimensions."

"But how do I understand what the dreams are trying to tell me?" Martika asked.

"How do you know they are trying to tell you anything at all?" Tía Tellín replied.

Martika considered for a moment then said, "I know what a regular dream feels like. These dreams are different. I feel like all my senses are on alert, more intense. The dreams of the jungle, and the smell of fire? Those make me feel like I need to figure something out. But the other dreams, in the dirty room—"

Tía Tellín interrupted her. "The ones where you feel as if you are inside someone else's mind?"

"Yes. Those don't make me feel like I'm supposed to *do* something, they just scare me."

Tía Tellín explained. "They feel different because they are a different kind of dream. Your instinct is correct. When you feel a sense of urgency, the dream is indeed trying to tell you something. Don't be afraid. Ask for guidance, ask for the answer."

"And the others?"

"You are dreaming the experience of the girl who was kidnapped, whose bracelet triggered the images in your mind. What you are experiencing is commonly found in twins, where they have a psychic link to each other. It can happen with strangers as well. Sometimes you meet a person and you feel as if you've known him a long time. Or you meet them first in a dream and then they show up in your waking life. Whatever it is, the dreams you have about Jennifer are important because she is in danger."

"How can my dreams help Jennifer?" Martika asked, confused.

Tía Tellín looked at her solemnly and said, "When the dream feels as if you are in someone else's mind, you are. You are dreaming Jennifer's reality and when you do, it is a sign that she is still alive."

Martika did not respond. The gravity of Tía Tellín's words hung in the air. Tía Tellín continued, "Keep a dream journal, starting tomorrow. Record whatever you remember upon waking, and we will work together to decipher its meaning. Soon you will learn how to interpret your own dreams. That is the first step in shamanic transformation."

She walked to the tall bookcase. She climbed a stepladder and removed a volume from the top shelf. It was large and its leather binding was cracked but polished. Its cover was worn in places and the spine had been repaired many times.

"This book holds the story of our people. You will read about the first gods, who added their own blood to the maize to make man. Our history began thousands of years ago. There were many powerful gods, many powerful cities and urban centers. Our rulers were divine kings, the god-kings who communed with the spirits. The supreme deity was Itzamná and his wife was Ixchel."

Martika interrupted. "I read about her today at school. There was a statue of her with a snake headband and a skirt made of crossbones."

"Ixchel is a powerful deity. She is the great mother of our people, the goddess of weaving, medicine, and childbirth. The sacred women who followed her wisdom lived in the nunnery with our ancestor Xusita. I want you to read as much as you can before our next session."

Martika reached for the book, but Tía Tellín hesitated for a moment.

"Remember what happened with Jennifer's bracelet?"

"Yes?"

"Be prepared."

As soon as Martika touched the book, a flood of images came into her mind. She shut her eyes.

A dense, humid jungle . . . many people seated in a circle as muscular men, painted in different colors and wearing spotted jaguar pelts, danced in the center . . . rhythmic drumming and smoke filled the air. The images faded into one another and a tall, dark-haired woman with amber eyes held out a transparent sphere, a ball of light, to Martika. The woman drew closer and the ball burst into flame, a whirling vortex of fire. . . .

Martika felt Tía Tellín's hand on her shoulder, pulling her back to her present reality. She heard her aunt's steady voice say, "This book has been handed down through many generations of *curanderas* in our family. When I was young, my grandmother gave it to me. Each night I would read it late into the night, learning about who I was and what I was to become."

Martika opened her eyes. Excited, she recounted her vision. "I saw people seated in a circle. There were drummers and dancing. The air smelled like smoke."

"You were in the jungle of your ancestors, *mija*." Tía Tellín looked pleased as she walked Martika to the door.

"And there was a dark-haired woman who handed me a ball of fire. Who was she?"

Tía Tellín stopped short at Martika's words. In her mind she heard the whispering voices.

Soraya . . .

"Tía?"

Tía Tellín opened the door. "She was one of your ancestors, of course. There have been many. Now hurry home and do your schoolwork. We will have a full afternoon of study tomorrow." Martika left, tucking the large volume under her arm.

In the parlor, Tía Tellín stopped at the mantel. She looked at a faded black-and-white photo of a young woman wearing clothes from the turn of the century. Her dark hair was pulled back at the nape of her neck. Her pale eyes stared at the camera with intensity; in her hand she held a transparent sphere. Tía Tellín looked at the image. It was the same woman Martika had seen in her vision. In her mind Tía Tellín spoke the words across the dimensions, to the otherworld: *Por Dios, Soraya . . . do not give her your terrible gift.*

Eight

❀

*T*he sun was just coming up as Ted gunned the engine of his Mercedes down Pacific Coast Highway. DiCario had gotten the rundown on the Hayes estate in Point Dume. Ted was convinced the statue of the jaguar was somewhere on the property; Hayes was known for keeping his impressive art collection there.

Hayes isn't so different from Eddie Blasi, Ted thought as he flew past Paradise Cove and Malibu proper. They were two guys who had figured out how to work the system and the people in it. In many ways Ted knew he wasn't so different from them; they just played on a bigger field, with higher stakes.

He couldn't shake off the guilt that had plagued him since Jennifer's abduction. *"It's your fault—it's because of you,"* Nancy had shouted at him in her drunken rage.

In his heart, he knew she was right. If he hadn't double-crossed Eddie Blasi, none of this would have happened. Luckily, Nancy had checked herself in to the Four Seasons Hotel and, apart from a handful of agitated phone calls each day, he hadn't seen her again. By late afternoon the calls usually stopped and he figured she was probably well on her way to drunk by then.

Ted pulled up to the gates of the Point Dume Estates. He kept his sunglasses on as he rolled down the window. "I'm here to see Mr. Herold," he said to the guard.

Bob Herold was a major-label record producer. Back in the eighties when Ted was running drugs for the Hollywood crowd, Bob had been one of his best clients. A quick phone call was all that was necessary to get clearance into the exclusive enclave of the Point Dume Estates.

The guard raised the gate arm, and Ted maneuvered the car around quiet streets with names like Via Hacienda and Via del Mar. High above the Pacific, the neighborhood had an unspoiled view of the ocean and the rugged cliffs of the point. There were no sidewalks, just lush, overflowing gardens set against vast expanses of lawn, all surrounded by walls and gates. Ted checked the directions DiCario had given him and hung a right on Via Marina. He saw the Hayes estate looming before him.

It was white granite, with an angular, modern design and a sprawling layout of connecting buildings. It sat on a bluff, and a steep stone stairway led down to the pristine beach below. A high wrought-iron fence ringed the property, and Ted could see the strategically placed security cameras at the perimeter. He parked his car and watched.

After a few minutes he saw a member of Hayes's security patrol, a muscular, black-clad man with a firearm strapped to his side. A large, fawn-colored German shepherd walked briskly beside him, eyes and ears alert. Ted wondered how he was possibly going to get past the security detail. Even if he did, how would he ever find the jaguar inside the huge house? He felt his resolve falter but he knew he couldn't give up; Jennifer's life depended on it.

Sitting in his car, watching the morning haze burn off and the sun begin to break through, Ted thought of his daughter. He knew he hadn't been a good father. Or a good husband. All he was good at was making money and hanging out with the people who could help him in that pursuit. Nancy had begun to drink when her loneliness became too much to bear. He thought back to all the canceled plans, all the nights he'd come home late to find his wife watching another old movie, drinking a scotch and soda. Usually Jennifer was asleep on the couch next to her, waiting for a father who never seemed to show up on time, if at all.

Since the divorce he'd tried to make up for his absence with a credit card in Jennifer's name, a new car, and all the latest things a teenage girl could want. But none of that counted for anything now. He looked at the gated, high security Hayes estate, knowing he had to get inside and find the jaguar. He had to get his daughter back safely.

Martika ran down the stairway and out to the street, her hair still wet. She had stayed up late reading Tía Tellín's book and had dreamed of the Mayan gods whose name filled her mind as she drifted to sleep. Hurakan, Itzamná, Ixchel, Chac, Kinich-Ahau. She'd overslept and now had to race to catch up with Lola for their walk to the bus stop. A glance at her watch showed 7:55. Good, she would make it on time and find out how dinner at Pepa's had been. Lola hadn't called and hadn't come over for dinner the night before, proving that Lola was acting weird. Everyone knew that Pepa's mother was a terrible cook; her *carne asada* was like eating the sole of an old shoe.

When Martika arrived at the fountain, no one was there. She looked around, expecting to see Lola, but all she saw was some homeless men emerging from the bushes. She waited ten, then fifteen minutes. By 8:15 she knew Lola wasn't coming.

Ever since Martika had changed schools two years ago, they had walked to the bus together. If one of them was going to miss it, she would call the night before. Now there was no Lola and there had been no call.

Maybe I shouldn't have told her about any of it, Martika thought as she walked slowly toward the bus stop. But how could she not have told Lola something so important? They had been best friends since first grade, when Lola defended Martika after some third graders knocked her down during a game of dodgeball. They had shared everything: playing Indians in the Thanksgiving pageant in fourth grade, the first day of middle school, the first time they each got their period and Lola had cramps that were so bad she had to get a shot from Dr. Irigoyen. They hung together when Lola's parents were out of work during the janitors' strike and Aurelia prepared extra food to send over to the Lopez house. When Martika's parents separated last year Lola was there, giving Martika tissues and a pep talk while they watched Camiso load up his truck and drive away.

Martika couldn't figure out what was going on with Lola—her strange attitude the day before, not coming to dinner, and now this.

Nothing has changed, she thought as she boarded the bus. But she knew she was only trying to convince herself. Since she had gone to Tía Tellín's house that first day, everything had changed.

A cockroach darted across the cracked bathroom tile. Like everything else in the building, the bathroom looked as if it hadn't been used for years. The water and electricity had been cut off, so Mojito had given Jennifer a large bottle of water to clean up with. She leaned over the sink and poured it into her hair. The lather from the bar of deodorant soap that Mojito left dripped into her eyes, stinging them. She felt grungy but was too scared to bathe, what with a guard on the other side of the door. She brushed her teeth and put on the other change of clothes they had given her, a baggy pair of second-hand jeans and a faded Seattle Seahawks T-shirt. Outside in the hallway she could hear her guard, a new gang recruit, shuffling impatiently.

"I'll be out in a minute," she called through the closed door.

She climbed onto the sink and pulled herself up to the window, high on the wall. She looked at the tops of other abandoned buildings and down to the weed-filled lot below. Broken bottles and trash littered the area. She pushed on the bars but they held fast. Disappointed, she climbed down, gathered her meager toiletries into a plastic grocery bag, and opened the door to the hallway.

The guard, Javier, stood against the wall, his hair newly shorn, wearing the trademark blue Dickies and a T-shirt. He followed Jennifer down the hall to her holding room. As they passed through the doorway he looked at her T-shirt and said, "Lousy team."

Jennifer looked up, surprised. *Maybe I can draw him out further*, she thought.

"I know. They could have at least gotten me a Steelers shirt," she said.

"You follow football?" he asked.

"I'm a cheerleader at school. Don't I look like one?" she replied with a wry smile.

Javier laughed quietly and said, "Well, yeah, you do."

She sat back down on the thin mattress and he took his place in the folding chair. They sat in silence for a long while. Jennifer looked at him from the corner of her eye. Javier was cute in a boyish way. He had straight white teeth and still had a layer of baby fat. His brown eyes moved restlessly as if he were always waiting for something to come up behind him. Finally Jennifer asked, "How long have you been in Mojito's gang?"

"A long time," he lied. He had joined recently and so far he hadn't had to do anything really bad. He was just keeping an eye on this rich white girl while Mojito and Blasi made a deal with her father. He looked at her now, her long blond hair drying in the air, the baggy clothes hanging off her slender frame.

"I bet you don't have any gangs out where you live."

"Not really. But we have a lot of rich kids who like to dress and act like they're in one."

Javier laughed out loud. She was sharp, even if she was a *niña mimada*. "I don't get that. Rich white kids acting all street, like they're from the barrio. They ought to try *living* down here, being jacked all the time. Then we'll see how cool they think it is!"

She smiled at his observation. He was obviously a lot more

on the ball than Kiko or Mojito. They fell into silence again.

After a while she said, "I hope my dad works it out with whoever arranged to have me kidnapped."

Javier knew he wasn't supposed to talk to her, but it was awfully boring to sit in silence. He figured there wasn't any real harm in talking to pass the time.

"I'm sure he's going nuts, calling the cops and everyone. He's probably called the governor! That's what my dad would do if someone took my sister."

"You have a sister? How old?" Jennifer asked.

"Fifteen."

"I just turned sixteen. What's her name?"

"Lola," replied Javier.

They heard the rumble of Mojito's Mustang outside and the sound of heavy footsteps on the stairs. Jennifer whispered nervously to Javier. "That's Mojito. I'm going to pretend to be asleep, okay?"

Javier was reluctant to go along. He didn't want to start keeping things from his *jefe*, not when he was trying to prove himself to his homies. Jennifer pleaded with him. "Please? He scares me when he comes by all jacked up like that."

Javier knew what she meant. Mojito was always wound up on something, and there were times when he scared Javier, too. They could hear his singsong whistle, and Jennifer lay down on the mattress and turned her face to the wall. The door opened and Mojito came in. Javier stood to greet him.

"*¡Hola, jefe!*" Mojito walked to Jennifer and leaned over her. She kept her eyes tightly shut, her breathing even. He whispered to Javier, "She's sleeping?"

Javier lied. "Yeah, she's been asleep for about an hour."

Jennifer's heart jumped. *Javier had covered for her!*

Mojito looked at her again, her long, wet hair splayed out on the mattress.

"She cleaned up, yeah?" Again Javier nodded. Mojito stepped closer to Javier and gave him a knowing look. Mojito leaned in and asked, "You didn't sneak a look at her, did you? Didn't just peek through the crack in the bathroom door?"

Mojito's eyes were smiling, but underneath them Javier could sense something menacing. He whispered, "No way, *jefe*. She's not my type."

Mojito patted him on the shoulder. "Good, *mijo*. That's good. Come out to the hall."

Jennifer heard their muffled voices, talking. She opened her eyes and took a deep breath. Maybe there was a chance to escape. Maybe Javier would help her.

Nine

❁

"So who wants to go to the blackboard to solve homework problem number eight?" Ms. Loftus, the geometry teacher, looked around the room for a victim. Martika hadn't done her homework the night before. She had gotten too caught up in reading Tía Tellín's book. She tried to slink down in her chair without calling attention to herself. Ms. Loftus had an eagle eye for students trying to get out of answering a question. Martika knew she had to play it just right, show interest and project the image of confidence, as if she had all the answers right there on the empty page of her notebook. Ms. Loftus scanned the room and her eyes lingered for a moment on Martika.

Please, God, don't let her call on me. . . . Mentally Martika went through the list of things she would give up or start doing if her prayer was answered.

"How about you, Miss Ling."

Ms. Loftus had called on Cristina Ling, a petite, studious girl who sat next to Martika. Cristina Ling walked to the blackboard with confidence. She had the answer; she always had the answer. As Cristina wrote out a proof in a perfect, neat hand, the bell rang. Martika swore to catch up on her homework over lunch.

Out on the quad, Martika grabbed a quesadilla from the lunch line and made her way to the study hall. Inside she found a cubicle and took out last night's unfinished homework. She was halfway through her social science chapter when her eyes grew heavy. She put her head down to rest and promptly fell asleep. A series of images flashed through her mind as she sank into dreaming:

Ms. Loftus at the blackboard . . . the soccer game on television the night before . . . the bus ride to school that morning. . . .

The images dissolved into one another, and suddenly she was back in Jennifer's house. Her senses were heightened, her nerves on edge. She knew immediately that this was not a regular dream. She tried to run to the pool house, but she seemed to be moving in slow motion. She pushed open the doors and walked inside, going right to the battered box tied with twine. There was tingling at the base of her skull. She remembered Tía Tellín's words, "Don't be afraid. Ask for guidance, ask for the answer . . ."

What I am looking for? she asked silently. She reached into the box and touched a hard object. The black newsprint of the packing paper rubbed off on her hands. She looked over her shoulder, knowing she had to open the package before someone arrived . . . but who? She couldn't get a grip on the object; it seemed to have fallen deeper into the box, just out of her reach. The tingling got stronger until it was an uncomfortable pulsing in her brain, and she heard the whispering of many voices.

She rose to her knees and leaned over the box, reaching in farther. The object had to be there . . . she felt herself pulled into the box. She fell into a fathomless blackness, tumbling head over heels, her arms flailing. She saw vague shapes in the darkness: amber-golden eyes of a big, spotted cat staring at her from the shadows. The jaguar.

He moved beside her, above her. Her eyes followed him as he moved below her. She looked down and saw a raging wall of fire leaping up to meet her as she fell faster and faster. The jaguar jumped over her, his body magnificent and powerful, his jaws open wide. He let out an ear-splitting screech. She reached out for him, desperate to grab on to his powerful back and be spirited to safety. As her fingers closed around his slick, spotted fur . . .

Martika jolted awake. The dream had been so real that for a moment she didn't recognize where she was. Then she saw the familiar bank of fluorescent lights hanging overhead and the study hall cubicles. She closed her eyes again and tried to imagine the scene she had been in. She was scared but she knew there was an important message in the dream. A message she could not understand. She felt a flash of anger at her father for forbidding her to be trained in the ways of the *curanderas* for so long. What right did he have to keep her from understanding her inheritance? After all, it was her gift, her responsibility. She felt useless and frustrated. Her best friend was tripping out and had stood her up. Now she had this terrifying dream that she couldn't figure out. The bell rang, bringing the lunch hour to an end, and she had not made a dent in her overdue homework. The day was going from bad to worse.

Martika got off the bus and trekked up the hill to Tía Tellín's house. She had done more research in Ms. Osser's class and had learned about the many Mayan kings who bore the name Jaguar. Bird Jaguar and Shield Jaguar, who each ruled the city of Yaxchilán. Then there was the famous jaguar throne at Palenque. It seemed the jaguar was everywhere in the history of the Maya. Now he had been in her dream, too.

She saw a car parked in the driveway of her aunt's house. It was the same dark sedan she and Lola had seen picking Tía Tellín up from the park. Maybe now she would learn who drove the mysterious car. Martika knocked. Tía Tellín opened the door and led her into the parlor.

A heavy-set, balding man in his fifties sat on the couch, holding a delicate teacup in his large, calloused hands. He wore a plain brown suit and a rumpled white shirt. He had a sheen of perspiration on his face; his eyes were deep and weary. He rose when Martika entered.

"This is my niece, Martika, the one I told you about," Tía Tellín said to the man.

"Nice to meet you, young lady. I'm John Guest."

"Martika Gálvez," she replied as she settled into the couch.

Who is this man and what is he doing here? She thought perhaps he was a *curandero*, but he looked more like a guy from the Hollywood Lanes bowling league than a shaman. She knew Tía Tellín must have read her thoughts when Tía glanced at Martika, suppressing a smile.

"Mr. Guest is a detective. He works out of the Rampart Division. I asked him to come by so you could tell him about the missing girl."

Martika looked uncertainly at Tía Tellín. Ted had said no police. Should she tell the detective about the dreams? And about Jennifer's bracelet? He felt her reluctance and said softly, "Your aunt has told me about your gifts, Martika. I've worked with her on a number of cases over the years. She has been a great help when we've hit a dead end in an investigation."

Martika looked at Tía Tellín, surprised. "You work with the police?"

Tía Tellín replied modestly, "From time to time."

"As a psychic?" Martika turned to Detective Guest.

"Yes," he replied, "and believe me, it's not something they talk about openly in the department. A lot of the younger guys don't believe in it. But I've seen what your aunt can do. She tells me you can, too."

Martika looked to Tía Tellín, who gave her a reassuring nod.

"Well, this girl, Jennifer Colton, was kidnapped last weekend," Martika said.

"Has her family filed a police report?" asked Detective Guest.

"No, the father says he was told to keep the police out of it."

Detective Guest took out a notebook and wrote down some information.

"What else do you know?"

"Just that she was taken from the house in the middle of the night and then . . ." she paused.

Detective Guest leaned in. "You had a dream, right? That's what your aunt said."

"Yes. I had a dream." Martika told him about the abandoned building, feeling as if she were in someone else's mind, and of her most recent dream of being stalked by a jaguar.

"And every time, I get this strange tingling at the base of my skull," Martika said.

"Your power is being stirred. When something connects with you on the psychic plane, you feel it as a tingling. Something important is in that box," Tía Tellín explained.

"But what about the fire?" Martika asked.

The old woman glanced quickly to Detective Guest, and Martika realized there were some things Tía Tellín could reveal only when he was not present.

Detective Guest took the cue. As he was leaving he said, "If her family had filed a proper police report, I could get a warrant and search the premises. But I can run a check on her father. The name is Colton, right? Like the car dealerships?"

"That's him."

On the porch Martika asked, "If that's your car, then you're the one who picks my aunt up every week?"

"I've been getting her help on a case. But like I said, it's very hush-hush. Don't go spreading it around the neighborhood. It's better if no one knows."

"That's right," Tía Tellín said with a smile. "Let them think I'm going to a bingo game or something."

Detective Guest shook Martika's hand and got into his car. "I'll be in touch," he said.

Martika turned to Tía Tellín. "So you're like the character on *Medium*? A police psychic?"

"I just help when I can."

"What case are you working on?"

"Confidential. That's one of the first things you have to learn. You have to guard your secrets, your power. It is far better for people to think you are an ordinary teenage girl so as not to attract any attention that might get in your way later."

"I guess so. Look at you—you look like someone's nice *abuelita*, and here you are, a crime fighter."

Tía Tellín laughed. "You make me sound like a comic book hero."

"There should be a comic about you. They could call it Super Abuela and you could read everyone's mind."

Tía Tellín shook her head in amusement as she steered Martika back into the house and closed the door behind them. They had serious work ahead of them.

Ted waited outside the Malibu realty office, sipping his third espresso. He had spent the day chatting up local residents, posing as a developer, trying to get whatever information he could on the Hayes house. He located the real estate agent who had listed it when Hayes bought it. Her name was Marni Fields and she was also known for dating some of the enclave's wealthy bachelors.

The coffee was bitter and Ted's nerves were jumpy from too much caffeine. He waited, leaning conspicuously on his black Mercedes. A red BMW pulled into the parking lot, and a long-legged blonde in Prada stepped out and headed into the realty office. It had to be her—she fit the description he had been given to a T. Ted watched her settle in at her desk before he entered and approached her with a smile. "Ms. Fields?"

"Yes?" She looked up and gave him an appraising glance, typical of an L.A. woman. He knew he was being sized up for the signals he was giving off: expensive clothes, Rolex watch, Mercedes-Benz key ring. He saw her take it all in as she came out from behind her desk with her manicured hand outstretched. He took it graciously.

"I'm Jack Riddell. I'm building some homes out near Trancas, and there's a house here in the Point Dume Estates that has really captured my attention. I was told you were the listing agent."

"Probably. That is my specialty area. Which home?"

"The large white one, out on the bluffs."

"Oh, the Hayes estate. I sold it to Mr. Hayes several years ago. It's an incredible piece of property. You're planning on building something similar? For you and your family, perhaps?"

Ted took the bait and answered, "I'm not married. I'm planning on building a series of estate homes; I bought up quite a bit of acreage."

Now she smiled and leaned in to him. "I'll give you as much information as I can about the home. I have the layout brochure here in one of my files." She moved to her filing cabinet and pulled out a glossy brochure of the home, complete with an architectural layout of the interior.

"It's really impressive, incredible flow to the interior, great for entertaining. . . ."

✹   ✹   ✹

Several hours later, Marni excused herself to use the ladies' room at Granita, and Ted checked his watch. It had been a productive day. Over several glasses of white wine, Marni had explained the floor plan of the house, told him where the art collection was kept, and even divulged some of R.J. Hayes' personal habits. She had dated him briefly and it had not ended well, so she was more than willing to spill some vindictive beans, especially after a few drinks. Ted now knew that R.J. Hayes was a meticulous control freak who had a schedule worthy of the Third Reich for his staff of domestic help. Ted even knew which doggie doors were popular with the guard dogs and which were not.

Useful information, he thought when Marni returned, her gait a little tipsy from the wine. The waiter arrived with the next round as she settled into her chair and gave Ted's hand a squeeze. He smiled and raised his glass to hers, ready to hear anything else she had to say about R.J. Hayes and his big white mansion on the bluff.

Ten

❁

*T*ía Tellín climbed the polished stairway, talking over her shoulder to Martika.

"For our people and for many other cultures around the world, the dreamtime is not just about unloading the day's events like a pile of old tortillas. The dreamtime is when you connect with the Great Spirit that infuses all of life. So now you must begin to learn how to set up your sacred space to enter the dreamtime at will. You cannot do it when you are distracted by everyday concerns."

They walked down the hallway. Downstairs Tía Tellín's house looked like any old-fashioned elderly grandmother's house. But when Martika followed her into the back bedroom, it didn't look like a grandma's house anymore. Woven rush mats covered the floor of Tía Tellín's spirit room. There were two rough-hewn chairs made of thick saplings. Carved wooden masks, painted in the images of animals, hung on the walls: masks of ocelots, tapirs, *chachalacas*. The largest was the jaguar. Its yellow and black paint was chipped in spots, the wood smooth and worn. It looked very old, as if it had passed through many hands and many lives before it came to hang on Tía Tellín's wall.

Martika saw an assortment of drums, some shaped like alligators and other animals. Soon she would learn their names, the two-toned *tunkul* and *zacatán* drums. There were *bubalek* and *kuyum* drums, small clay whistles shaped like insects, bone raspers, and gourd rattles. A tall rain stick made from a hollow tree branch filled with small pebbles and shell fragments leaned in a corner. In a large glass cupboard there were carefully labeled jars of herbs and powders, as well as long stalks of fresh herbs drying upside down to retain their potency. Candles with the images of saints on them burned in tall glass holders, their flames flickering in the quiet of the room. The air smelled of smoke and sage. Martika stood mesmerized.

"You will get used to all of this in time, Martika. If your father had allowed you to begin your training earlier, you would have been coming to this room since you were able to walk. And the names and uses of the herbs would be second nature to you. But you will learn quickly, I have no doubt."

Martika had enough doubt for twenty people and she didn't see how she was ever going to learn to be a real *curandera*.

"Eventually you will have your own spirit room, your own

sacred space. For now you must build an altar, no matter how humble. It will be the place you use to focus your power, your energy."

Tía Tellín pointed to her own altar. It held photos of friends and family members who had died and small plates of food and drink honoring them, inviting their spirits to return. There were vases of fresh flowers and glasses of water and beer. Clay figures of the Mayan deities stood in the center of the altar: the sun god and his counterpart the jaguar; the Bacabs, gods of the four directions who support the earth; and a large statue of the powerful moon goddess, Ixchel.

"What should I put on mine?" Martika asked. She had seen the Day of the Dead altars that her relatives made. Every November 1 her aunt Hortensia went to Forest Lawn Cemetery and put food, drink, and marigolds on the grave of her uncle Enrique.

"You will put candles of the saints to whom you have a special connection, photos of your relatives who have passed over and are watching from the other side, and photos of your loved ones and friends who walk with you in this life. You are young, so put images of the dreams you have for your life, your aspirations . . . and the icons of power that are yours alone."

From her altar Tía Tellín took a soft velvet bag the color of eggplant and handed it to Martika.

"Open it, " Tía Tellín said.

Martika pulled the drawstring and took out three small

stone statues. One was of Ixchel and the other two were of Itzamná, the supreme deity of the Maya, and of the powerful Balam-Agab, the jaguar god of the night. Tía Tellín explained, "I have been keeping them for years, hoping that someday I would give them to you. When a *curandera* in our line passes to the otherworld, her talismans of power are guarded until the next in the line is born. Those talismans are then given to the next one who carries the gift."

Martika turned them over in her hands. They were heavy and smelled of the earth. Martika felt the tingling sensation.

"Who did these belong to?" she asked

"They belonged to my mother's sister, Soraya. She was a very powerful *curandera*. She could do things unknown to our line before her."

"Like what?"

Tía Tellín paused, then said, "She had the gift of pyrokinesis; she was a firestarter. It had never been part of our legacy before or since."

Martika thought of the dream where she was falling into a wall of fire. She remembered holding Tía Tellín's book and the vision of the beautiful, dark-haired woman who tried to hand her the burning sphere.

"You mean Soraya could start fires with her mind?"

Tía Tellín nodded. "It was a defensive gift. She came into it at a difficult time. Our land had been taken from us. Our customs had been destroyed in the name of progress and assimilation. Soraya created a wall of fire to help us flee and find a safe place to hide and live. She struck terror in the hearts of those who wanted to harm us. I remember well; I was a small child. We called it Soraya's Fire, the time of the burning."

"Is she still alive? Can I meet her?"

Tía Tellín shook her head. "Soraya died when she was still a young woman, not yet thirty years old. She was consumed by her own gift."

Martika felt the weight of history, of the women who had carried this gift before her. The stone icons felt heavy in her hands and she asked, "Do you think the fire I saw in my dream could have something to do with Soraya? Or the vision of the woman with the sphere?"

Tía Tellín knelt down next to Martika and took her hand.

"Perhaps, but I want you to understand, Martika, you are powerful. Without any training at all you can do things that take years to learn. You must practice every day to strengthen those gifts, but you must not push for too much too soon. For now, focus your attention on your dream work. Learn to listen and understand what the dreams are telling you."

"And the fire?"

"I cannot say. Maybe it was a warning that you, too, have the gift of Soraya's Fire."

"How do I try it?" Martika asked, unable to hide the excitement in her voice.

Tía Tellín grasped her arm firmly. "You are *never* to try to use it. Do you understand me? You are untrained—you have to learn how to control you gifts, fine-tune them until you have developed subtlety and precision. If not, you will be unleashing a power that you cannot control."

Tía Tellín's eyes were fierce. Martika nodded silently.

Outside the sky was already dark. The candlelight threw ominous shadows on the masks that lined the walls. The jaguar's smile turned to a menacing grimace.

"For now, make your altar. Ask for a dream of guidance. You must find out what is in the mysterious box at Jennifer's house. That is the key."

By the time Martika had finished studying for her biology final, it was nearly midnight. She cracked open her door and peered out to the living room. Her mother was fast asleep while a rerun of *Corazón Salvaje* played on the late-night Spanish-language channel. Martika tiptoed to the kitchen to get the items for her altar. She filled a small juice glass with water and took a handful of pumpkin seeds from the cupboard.

Maybe the spirits would like something sweet? Martika wondered. She broke off a piece of dark chocolate from one of her mother's candy bars and snuck back into her room. She cleared off her dresser and placed the icons that Tía Tellín had given her in the middle of a circle of small candles. Then she added the tall candles in glass holders that her mother always bought at the 99 cent store and gave her for protection. They bore religious images of Jesus with *El Corazón Sagrado* and the Virgin of Guadalupe.

From her bedside table she took a small framed photo of Tata Manuel, her great-grandfather who died when she was a child, and a photo of Nana Maria, Aurelia's mother who passed just last year. She placed them among the candles, the glass of water and the edible treats. She found a photo of her parents from a trip they had taken together to Santa Barbara several years earlier, when they were still happy together. And a photo of Lola dressed up like Elvira for Halloween, and the cover of a *National Geographic* magazine about an archeological dig in Egypt.

Family, friends, her dreams for the future—she placed them all on her altar. She lit the candles and turned out the lights. In the darkness of her room, the candles threw shadows across the stone icons, illuminating them, animating them. She closed her eyes and pictured Jennifer as she had seen her in the photos in the Amalfi Drive house.

Where are you? she asked silently. She thought of the jaguar that had run beside her in her dream. *What are you telling me? What should I do?*

She opened her eyes and focused on the flame of a lit candle. What if she really had the gift of Soraya's Fire? Martika knew Tía Tellín had told her not to try it, but perhaps she could do it? She stared hard at the flame, trying to make it grow stronger. It danced and jumped in the breeze from the open window. Martika knew that the flame was just doing what it always did; she had no control over it at all. She climbed into bed, pulled up the covers, and stared at her altar across the small bedroom. Her eyes grew heavy and she told herself, *One day I will have learned all that I need to know . . . I will be powerful like Tía Tellín, like Soraya . . . a* curandera . . .

She slipped into sleep and did not see when a sudden gust of wind blew out all the candles except for the one illuminating the Balam-Agab, jaguar of the night.

Eleven

✿

"*A*y, mariposa de amor, mi mariposa de amor. Ya no regreso contigo . . .*" Maná sang on the clock radio, waking Martika from a deep sleep. She fumbled for the off button in the darkness. The clock read 4:30 A.M. She pulled a binder and pen from the bedside table to take notes on her dream.

> *By the ocean, tall cliffs behind her . . . she was running, as fast as she could to catch the jaguar. He ran effortlessly, his powerful limbs propelling him forward, his spotted fur rippling with the movement of his muscles. The chase was futile; she would never catch him. Suddenly he turned and faced her, his amber eyes reflecting the setting sun. She approached him and he sat still, waiting for her . . . waiting for her . . .*

She had hoped for a dream that was more obvious, maybe one that would tell her how to get into the box at Jennifer's house, but she was learning that her dreams didn't read like textbooks or recipes. They spoke a deeper language of her subconscious that she was just beginning to understand. Besides, she had come up with her own plan for getting into the box, but she couldn't think about that now. She slid the dream journal into her backpack, took out her geometry textbook, and began working on her overdue homework. She couldn't afford to be behind with finals coming up. The numbers on the page ran together and she rubbed her tired eyes. She *had* to focus on her schoolwork.

Two hours later, she heard a knock at her bedroom door.

"Are you up already, *mija*? It's not seven yet," her mother asked.

"I got up early to finish my homework," Martika replied.

Aurelia leaned against the doorway, her faded chenille bathrobe pulled around her. She raised an eyebrow when she noticed Martika's dresser, the icons and candles with their singed wicks.

"Did Tía Tellín show you that?" she asked.

"It's my altar," Martika said self-consciously.

"Nothing wrong with that, honey. It's part of being a *curandera*. They all have them. Just don't burn the place down. And make sure your father doesn't see it . . . and one more thing, no chicken blood in this house, okay?"

Martika made a face. "That's disgusting, mom!"

"I saw that movie with Robert De Niro and that crazy actor who boxes . . . *Angel Heart* it was called."

"That was about Santería."

"I don't know how it all works. I'm just saying . . . *no sangre de gallina*," Aurelia said with a wink as she shuffled down the hallway toward the kitchen.

A few moments later, Martika brushed past her, grabbing an apple and a banana on her way out.

"Where are you going so early?" Aurelia asked.

"Got some things to take care of before school!" Martika called over her shoulder.

"Is Lola meeting you?" Aurelia's voice carried to the stairway.

"Yeah, but she doesn't know it yet!" Martika shouted her reply, hoping she woke up the Mendez family and their six hot-water-using kids.

Martika walked briskly across the park, passing the fountain without stopping. Today she wasn't waiting. If something was bothering Lola, then Martika was going to find out what it was. This was no way for best friends to act.

When she arrived at the large brick apartment building where Lola lived, Martika pushed the door open and took the stairs two at a time. She knocked on the door of apartment number seven. Lola's mother, Patricia, opened it.

"Hola, mija. ¿Que haces aquí tan temprano? ¿Todo está bien con tu mamá?"

"Hi, Mrs. Lopez. My mom is fine. Is Lola here?"

Patricia gestured to the bathroom.

"She's in the bathroom, getting ready. Where else would she be?"

Martika went to the bathroom door and knocked. Lola opened it, her makeup half done.

"Hey! What's up?" Lola said, looking embarrassed.

"The usual. What's up with you?

Lola turned back to the mirror to apply her mascara. "Nothing."

Martika sat on the edge of the bathtub. "So why didn't you come to the fountain yesterday? I waited for you."

"Oh, I was late and I went with Ramón." Ramón was Lola's older brother, a senior at Elysian.

"Since when do you go to school with Ramón? You never ride with him," Martika pressed her. Lola shrugged.

"And dinner the night before?" Martika asked.

"I just figured it was easier to stay at Pepa's . . ."

Martika reached out and took the mascara wand from her.

"Hey, it's me, your best friend. Why are you acting so strange? Is it because of what I told you about Tía Tellín?"

Lola pretended to arrange her makeup box for a beat and then replied, "Well, yeah. You tripped me out with that stuff! It's weird enough that you're related to the neighborhood *bruja*, but now you tell me that you're one, too!"

"Tía Tellín is not a *bruja*; she's a *curandera*."

"Whatever! She can read people's minds and see the future, can't she?"

"It's not just psychic stuff, Lola. It's about us, *all* of us. It's our history, where we come from."

Lola raised an eyebrow, skeptical. "Maybe it's *your* history 'cause you've inherited some weird-ass powers. But it's not mine. My parents are from Tijuana, girl, and my mom is no mind reader!"

"I mean there's a lot of history in it, a lot of incredible things I never knew before," Martika explained.

"But isn't it kind of creepy? You know, all that psychic stuff?" Lola asked.

"Well . . . yeah, in some ways. And a lot of it is really hard to believe. But Tía Tellín is the only person who seems to be able to make sense of what is going on with me. So I have to believe it," said Martika.

Lola was quiet a moment, then asked, "And what about that missing girl? Any news on her?"

"Yes. I had another dream about her house, and there's this box that I have to get into—"

Lola interrupted her. "Okay, this I don't understand. How can you be all involved in the life of this white girl you don't even know? Who is she to you?"

Martika looked at her for a moment and then it dawned on her.

"Are you jealous, Lola?"

Lola snorted as she turned to apply her lipstick. "Of course not! Why would I be jealous of that Jennifer, whoever she is?"

Martika broke into a wide smile. "You are so! That's why you're acting so weird!"

Lola set down the lipstick and turned to her. "Okay! I'm a little jealous. Here you have this special power, and it's tied to some girl you've never met who needs your help now that she's been kidnapped, so where does that leave me?"

Martika looked at her in the mirror and said, "Right where you've always been! You're my best friend, Lola. That hasn't changed."

"Are you sure?" Lola asked. "Maybe you're not going to be interested in normal things anymore? Maybe reading minds and seeing the future is going to make hanging out with me seem boring."

Martika laughed. "I can't do *any* of those things! All I'm learning is how to understand these crazy dreams and not to be freaked out by them."

"So you can't read my mind right now?"

"Of course not!"

Lola smiled sheepishly. "I guess it wouldn't matter anyway, 'cause I tell you everything."

"How's this? When and if I ever *can* read minds, I'll let you know and I won't read yours?"

"Deal!" Lola said. "So what's up with your wacko dreams?"

"I had a dream about a box I saw at Jennifer's house the day she was kidnapped. I have to find out what's in it. I have a plan. Tomorrow is a half day at school, so . . ."

There was a loud knock at the bathroom door. Lola's brother's annoyed voice carried through the wall, "*¡Ya, Lolita!* Enough with the *pinche maquillaje!*"

"I'm coming—*¡no seas grosero!*" Lola shouted back. They left the bathroom and passed Javier, who had been listening at the door. He watched them disappear into Lola's room. He overheard them talking about a girl named Jennifer who had been kidnapped. Could they have been talking about the same girl he had been guarding for Mojito? *No way,* he thought, closing the door behind him. The world couldn't be that small.

Jennifer rinsed her face with the remaining bottled water and dried it with toilet paper. She lingered in the dirty bathroom, taking advantage of the few minutes of privacy away from Kiko. It had only been five days but it seemed like forever. Having no contact with the outside world was beginning to drive her crazy; she felt so dependent and helpless. She heard a car and quickly climbed to the grate of the window to peer out. A sleek, black Jaguar pulled into the deserted lot and a tall, thin man with straw-colored hair stepped out.

A moment later Mojito came around the corner of the building and Jennifer leaned back, out of view. Could that be the man who had planned her kidnapping? They talked for a few moments and then she heard the thin man say, "I gave him seven days to get it back to me. If not, then we decide what to do with her."

Seven days? And then what?

Their voices dropped and she couldn't hear any more of their conversation. She thought of her father, always on the phone, making another deal or partying with his friends. Would Ted give the tall, thin man what he wanted in time? She hated to admit it, but in her heart she wasn't sure he would.

The car engine started up. Jennifer climbed down and leaned against the wall. She closed her eyes, trying to block out the words that kept repeating themselves again and again in her mind: *seven days.*

It was past nine P.M. when Detective Guest pulled off the 101 Freeway at Broadway. On his way home he had decided to take a detour into the industrial section of downtown. The place in Martika's dream about Jennifer was somewhere in this area; he was certain of it.

A tall building with a barred window high on the wall . . . it seems abandoned.

That's what Martika had described. He knew some of the other guys on the force would make fun of him for believing in the psychic dreams of a fifteen-year-old girl. But he did believe. And he couldn't just sit idly by knowing Jennifer had been kidnapped, even if it hadn't been reported.

He took a right onto Alameda. He drove slowly down the

deserted street, passing Union Station and the rows of boxcars waiting eerily on the train tracks. He drove through Little Tokyo and turned east, deep into the manufacturing district. He cruised the tall buildings with their windows boarded up and For Lease signs posted, looking for anything suspicious. The streets were dead quiet, but Guest knew that there was a whole world of activity in the alleyways and shadows. Homeless people bedding down, young drug dealers waiting to make a sale to the streetwise yuppies from across town.

In front of a row of brick buildings, he idled the car. The buildings were all in the same style, with barred windows on the upper floors. *Could this be the place?* he wondered.

He shut off the engine and got out. In the parking area behind the buildings, he saw fresh tire tracks in the dirt. Someone had been here recently. A low rider full of young men cruised by, flashing gang signs.

What am I doing here alone, at this hour? I'm not a young hot-shot anymore.

He had suffered a mild heart attack the year before and was just six months away from retirement. He was no match for a car full of young thugs looking for trouble. He'd go to his boss and try to get a warrant to search the building, with a couple of cops to back him up. As he walked back to his car, a large, greasy rat ran over his shoe and into a crack in the door of the building. Detective Guest looked up at the darkened windows and hoped Jennifer wasn't inside, for her own sake.

Twelve

❁

*A*t 1:15 the next day, Martika sat on the front stoop outside her apartment building holding a bag from the local 99 cent store and a large Rubbermaid bin. She had spent the night before studying Tía Tellín's book and refining her plan for today. A 1996 Ford Fiesta came around the corner with Lola sitting in the backseat. Her brother Ramón was at the wheel. At eighteen, he was tall and lanky, his black, curly hair cropped short. He was more classically handsome than his younger brother, Javier, with strong Indian features and long eyelashes framing his dark eyes. Martika had known him most of her life; she was like another little sister to him. The car stopped and Lola leaned out.

"He's gonna be our chauffeur and drive the get-away car!" she said. Martika climbed in and elbowed Ramón.

"How'd Lola convince you to drive?'

"She promised to give me the first shot at the shower so I don't have to wait for her daily makeup ritual. And I pulled a hamstring so I can't practice." He was the captain of the soccer team at Elysian as well as the academic decathlon squad.

"What's up with the container?" asked Lola.

"It's part of my plan to get inside the house," Martika replied.

Ramón got in line for the freeway on-ramp and asked, "Okay, so what's going on here? All Lola told me is that you have to go to some house in the Palisades."

Before Martika could answer, Lola spoke up. "Here's the story: Martika has psychic powers, this rich girl has been kidnapped, and we have to get into a special box to help find her."

"Have you kids been watching too many cartoons? Maybe reading those old Nancy Drew mysteries from the library?" he asked, merging into the freeway traffic.

Lola punched him in the arm. "Who're you calling 'kids'?"

Ramón looked at Martika.

"Anything you want to add to that story, Martika? 'Cause I'm not driving an hour across town for some sci-fi channel nonsense."

"It's not that simple, Ramón, but it's true. I've been having telepathic dreams and episodes of, well . . . psychic activity," Martika said.

"Really? How do you know they were telepathic or psychic? Did the spirits communicate with you? Like the Haunted

Mansion at Disneyland?"

Lola leaned in from the backseat. "It's real. Tía Tellín is teaching her and she even had her talk to a detective from the police!"

At the mention of Tía Tellín and the police, Ramón stopped joking.

"Listen, if you two have gotten me involved by having me drive, I need to know what this crazy scenario is. And believe me, if I wasn't tired of computer games, I wouldn't be here. So, *suelta la lengua, chica.*"

He looked at Martika expectantly. She took a deep breath. "It all started a few weeks before my *quinceañera*. . . ."

Ted sat with Mike DiCario, going over the layout of the Hayes estate. They had the diagrams. Several of Ted's crew hovered nearby, waiting for instructions.

"Marni said that this entrance, off the kitchen, is where most of the help enters and exits. Hayes doesn't like them coming in the front door," Ted said.

"Are these French doors alarmed on the days the house-keepers are there?" DiCario asked, taking notes.

"No. The housekeeping staff comes over four times a week. Same with the service that cares for the houseplants and the dog trainer, Ilse. She takes the guard dogs down to the beach for training."

DiCario looked uncertain. "You want us to get into the

house in the middle of the day? With all that activity?"

Ted sat back in his chair and rubbed his tired eyes. "I think all the activity works in our favor. Doors will be open, people coming and going. At night the whole place will be on lockdown with Hayes out of town. During the day, the security staff might be less vigilant."

DiCario didn't want to dash Ted's hopes, but he didn't think that there would ever be a moment when the ex-cons guarding Hayes's house would be less vigilant. Ted insisted on going into the house himself. All DiCario and the other guys had to do was watch Ted's back and create some kind of distraction at the main entrance so he could get inside. And DiCario didn't see how Ted had a prayer of finding the jaguar, much less getting it out. But he knew Ted was desperate. *Maybe he'll get arrested for breaking and entering, and then we can get the police involved like we should have from the beginning,* DiCario mused as Nancy passed by en route to the kitchen. Ted had agreed to let her come by the house and to keep her in the loop as long as she stayed sober. So far, she had been sticking to Diet Coke and she seemed no worse for the ban on scotch.

DiCario rose and turned to his team. "We'll drive out now and get familiar with the property. We'll need to stake out the entrances and decide on everyone's positions."

Ted reached for his keys. DiCario put up a hand.

"No, Ted. You can't risk being seen out there again. You stay here with your ex-wife—try to get some rest."

After DiCario and his team left, Nancy emerged from the kitchen with a tall glass of soda. "Do you think you can do it?"

He looked at her squarely and replied, "I have to do it. So I will."

She smiled faintly, for the first time since her arrival in Los Angeles.

"I know you really love her, Ted. I'm sorry I said all those awful things."

Ted smiled back, grateful for Nancy's apology.

She said, "I'll get you a Diet Coke and we can sit outside by the pool, just chill for a while."

It was the best offer Ted had gotten in a long time.

Ramón turned the Fiesta onto Amalfi Drive and headed toward the Colton house. He couldn't believe Martika's story, but he knew her to be a girl who was intelligent, serious, and not prone to making up fantasies. He was still weighing it when Martika said, "This is it," pointing to the large Tudor.

Lola's jaw dropped open as she stared out the window. "Jennifer lives in that house with her father? Just the two of them?" she asked in disbelief.

"I know. Totally weird," said Martika.

"You're planning to sneak inside *that* house without being caught?" Ramón asked.

"I'm only going to sneak in if I have to. If Mr. Colton is home, he'll let us in," she said.

Martika reached for the plastic container and filled it with the contents of the bag from the 99 cent store: candy bars, boxes of tea, peanut brittle, and other items. Lola and Ramón look at her, puzzled.

"You know how kids are always knocking on doors or hanging outside supermarkets trying to sell stuff to get points for going to camp or something?" Martika asked.

"Yeah?" said Lola.

"So that's what we do. We knock on the door, we say our barrio is so bad, so many gangs, we have to sell this stuff to get a chance to go to the mountains."

"I've never been to the mountains!" said Lola.

"Good! Say that!"

"And then what?" Ramón asked.

"Then I ask if I can use the bathroom. And I check out the pool house while Lola keeps them talking."

"Doesn't he know what you look like?" asked Ramón.

Martika pulled a baseball cap out of her backpack and tucked her ponytail into it. She stuck her hand out to Ramón.

"Give me your glasses," she said.

Ramón took them off reluctantly, saying, "I can't see that well without them."

Martika put them on and blinked a few times, adjusting her eyes.

"I can't see that well *with* them so that makes two of us. But I can fake it. You can see to the corner, can't you?"

"Yeah. You want me to wait there?" he asked.

Martika grinned. "You're a natural at this, Ramón."

"What if there's no one home?" Lola asked.

"Then it's plan B. I sneak in through the yard. The back fence borders a ravine—there are no houses back there. If we're not out in about twenty minutes, come and look for us. Come on, Lola." The two girls climbed out and moved to the gate. Ramón watched them, doubtful. Martika waved him away toward the corner.

"Great," Ramón muttered as he pulled the car away.

Martika and Lola carried the Rubbermaid container between them, walked to the gate and pushed the buzzer. They waited for a long time and then heard Ted's voice crackle over the intercom.

"Who is it?"

Martika spoke up. "Hi! We're selling candy and other items as part of a drive to go to summer camp. We live in the inner city and our neighborhood youth group is sponsoring this drive to raise money. Would you be interested in buying some?"

"No thanks, honey," he answered dismissively.

Lola spoke up. "It's for a really good cause, mister. Our neighborhood is really bad with lots of gangs, and we have the chance to go camp outdoors in the mountains and get away from all those bad influences for a week."

Martika suppressed a laugh and whispered, "You go, girl!"

In the background they heard a woman's voice say, "Come

on, Ted. They're just kids. Give them a break."

Lola shot Martika a questioning glance. "*La* ex-wife," Martika mouthed silently.

After a moment, Ted said, "Okay. I'll buzz you in. Come to the front door."

The gate opened and they walked across the sprawling front yard. Lola gave a low whistle, impressed, as Martika pushed the doorbell. Ted and Nancy opened the door together.

"So what do you girls have to sell?" he asked.

Martika kept her eyes down while she rummaged through the candy and other goods. With Ramón's glasses on, all she could see was a wash of color.

"Well, we have candy bars and we have herbal tea and batteries . . ."

"Maybe some tea," Ted said.

"How about a Reese's peanut butter cup? Everyone likes those," Lola said.

Nancy crouched down to look into the bin. "Those are my daughter's favorite. How many do you have?"

Martika counted. "We have six."

"I'll take them all."

Ted looked at Nancy, surprised, and she said simply, "It'll be a nice treat for her when she comes home."

Martika knew it was time to make her move and asked, "Excuse me, would it be okay if I use your bathroom? We've been out here all day."

"Sure, honey. Down the hall on the right." Ted gestured toward the back of the house.

As she made her way down the hallway, she heard Lola's animated voice saying, "We're really excited because we get to go to the mountains, you know, sleep in sleeping bags, make s'mores . . ."

Martika moved quickly, pulling off Ramón's glasses and pocketing them as she headed toward the back of the house. She crossed the yard and prayed that the pool house was unlocked. The door opened easily. Inside, she looked under the counter but there was no box. She opened the cupboards under the sink and the closets but still, no box. Martika felt her nerves getting the best of her and she remembered Tía Tellín's words. *Calm your mind, clear your thoughts . . .*

She took a deep breath, closed her eyes, and let her mind go blank.

Where is it? she asked herself. *It has to be here.*

She moved to the bathroom cupboards and opened them, rifling through the white beach towels and cabana sheets, and then she saw it.

The box was open, the string cut.

She crouched down and reached into it but found nothing. She removed the newspaper and other packing material. The box was empty.

"What are you doing in here?"

Startled, Martika turned to face Ted. Behind him, Nancy stood with a terrified Lola. Ted asked again, his voice rising, "What are you doing in here? Who are you and what do you want?"

Nancy started toward the house. "I'm calling the police."

"No! Please don't!" Martika said. "I can explain. I'm Martika, Aurelia's daughter."

Ted looked confused, "Aurelia Gálvez? My housekeeper?"

Martika took off the baseball cap, letting her long ponytail fall out.

"Remember me? I was helping my mom the day Jennifer was kidnapped."

"What are you doing with that box? What do you know about it?" Ted asked angrily.

"I know this sounds crazy, Mr. Colton, but I've been having these dreams about her and I think this box has something to do with it—"

The doorbell sounded, interrupting her. On the closed-circuit security television, they saw Ramón at the front gate.

"I'll be right back. Don't move!" Ted ordered Martika and Lola. He disappeared and came back a few moments later with Ramón.

"What's going on?" Ramón asked. Martika handed him his glasses. Ted turned to Martika, his arms crossed, and said, "Go on with your story."

"I've been having these dreams, first about Jennifer and

then about this box. There was something in the box, something important."

Nancy looked at her suspiciously and said, "So what? Of course you had a dream about Jennifer. You knew she was kidnapped. That would scare any kid."

"It wasn't a normal dream," Martika explained. " I felt like I was inside her mind, I could see what she was seeing—"

Ted cut her off. "That's the craziest thing I've ever heard! How could you see what she was going through?"

Martika faltered. How could she bring up her psychic abilities without seeming like a lunatic? Suddenly Lola blurted out, "Martika is psychic, Mr. Colton. She can see things, visions and stuff."

Ted turned to Nancy. "This is a bunch of nonsense! Call the police!"

"Tell them about the bracelet, Martika!" Lola said.

"What bracelet? Did you take my daughter's bracelet?" Nancy asked.

"No!" Martika replied. "Mr. Colton asked my mom and me to come back, after Jennifer was kidnapped. Remember? You two had a big fight by the front door?" Ted and Nancy exchanged an embarrassed glance. Martika continued, "I went into Jennifer's room and I saw her bracelet, the one with the animals on it."

"It's her favorite. It was a gift from my mother," Nancy said.

"I picked it up and as soon as I held it, I saw images of Jennifer. It's called psychometry. It happens when you hold an object that belongs to someone. I saw Jennifer being carried out of the house in the middle of the night. Remember, Mrs. Colton? I talked to you on the stairs. I told you she was okay."

Nancy answered quietly. "Yes, I remember."

Ted remained unconvinced, his arms still folded across his chest. "What about the box?" he asked.

"There was something important in it. I felt it the day of your party, and I had a dream about it. I get a feeling at the base of my skull when something triggers my psychic abilities. It has to do with whatever was in this box."

"And?" Ted pressed her.

"It's all related to Jennifer being kidnapped."

Ted looked at her in silence. Her story sounded like something on *The X-Files*, but she was right about the box and its contents. The jaguar had been packed inside. Still doubtful, he took off his watch and handed it to Martika.

"Here. You say you can see images when you hold someone's personal objects? Tell me what you see about me," he challenged her.

Martika did her best to hide her anxiety as she took the watch. She didn't know how to control her gift, and she had never done it at will. If she wasn't able to call it up now, they would all get arrested for attempted burglary or something worse. She wrapped her fingers around the platinum Rolex and closed her eyes. She heard Tía Tellín's voice in her head.

You are powerful. . . . you can do things that take years to learn.

She cleared her thoughts. She moved the watch between her fingers and kept her mind blank. First she saw a light mist, like a slow fog rolling in. Then an image rose out of it. It was faint at first but then it became clearer. It was a teenage boy, a tall, dark-haired boy. He ran beside a car, holding fast to the door handle as the car pulled out of a driveway. The boy called out to the man inside the car, desperate. Martika took another deep breath, feeling the boy's panic. The boy was shouting, "Dad! Don't go! Don't leave me!"

The boy was Ted. Martika opened her eyes.

"He left you in the driveway," she said.

Ted looked at her, confused. "What are you talking about?"

"It was your dad. You held on to the door of his car. He drove away and left you," Martika said.

Ted blanched. He had never talked about the awful day his father abandoned him and his family. No one knew about it, not even Nancy. But Martika had seen it clearly, just the way it had happened. Now he knew she was telling the truth about the box and Jennifer.

The others all stared expectantly at Ted. He put his watch back on and his voice sounded rubbery and thick when he finally spoke. "You're right. I've never told anyone about that. There's no way you could possibly have known it."

Nancy took Martika's hand and said, "I'm so sorry. You

really saw my daughter? You think she's still alive?" Her voice cracked.

"Yes, I do," Martika said.

"Let's go inside and figure this out," said Ted, ushering Martika, Ramón, and Lola into the house. The three teens looked at one another, relieved.

Ted's mind was already working in overdrive. Even if he got into the Hayes house, he'd still have to find the jaguar and get out with it. The situation seemed hopeless, but maybe this extraordinary girl could help.

Thirteen

✿

Martika sat on a tall stool in Ted's kitchen and stared at the photo in front of her. It was a stone statue of a jaguar, about a foot tall. It was chipped in places and one of its teeth had broken off. Its eyes were set with precious stones.

"That's it, the cause of this whole nightmare," Ted explained. "A guy named Eddie Blasi was set to buy the statue, and I made a better deal with someone else. Now Blasi's holding Jennifer hostage until I get it back to him."

"Where is it now?" Martika asked.

"An art collector named R.J. Hayes bought it. It's somewhere in his estate, out in Malibu. I've made a plan to break into the house, find the statue, and take it back. And return his money, of course."

Martika passed the photo to Ramón.

"How are you going to get into the house and get the statue

out? The guy must have massive security," Ramón asked skeptically.

Ted said, "It's like the State Department. Armed guards, hi-tech security system, the whole thing." He showed them the sprawling layout of the house.

"This place makes your house look as tiny as mine, Mr. Colton. How are you going to find the statue once you're inside?" Martika asked.

"That's where I was thinking you might be able to help. If you go out to the Hayes house with me, maybe you could find the statue, using your . . . powers or whatever you call them."

Martika considered for a moment, then said, "Maybe I could—"

Ramón interrupted her. "I know you're in a bad situation, Mr. Colton, but this isn't some sci-fi movie. Martika could get into a lot of trouble or get hurt."

"Or worse," Lola said.

"When are you breaking into the Hayes house?" Martika asked Ted.

"In three days. Hayes has a staff that shows up to work on the same day; I know their schedule. I'll have all my guys and Mike DiCario, my private investigator, with me. They'll be staked out all around the perimeter of the property. We'd make our move from the back side of the house. Are you willing to help us, Martika?"

"If Martika is going, then I'm coming, too," said Lola.

"And me. To keep a lookout," said Ramón.

Martika looked at them, surprised. Lola smiled back at her and said simply, "Best friends watch your back, girl."

"This is crazy, Ted! You can't get all these kids involved in this mess! We have to call the police!" Nancy said, growing agitated.

Ted took her hand. "Honey, I can't do that. And not because of my business dealings; I don't care if I get into trouble. Blasi warned me, no police. This guy has eyes in back of his head. I'm sure he has this house wired. He probably knows what I'm going to do before I do."

Ted turned to Martika. "It's up to you, Martika. I'll talk to your mother and—

Martika cut him off. "No way! You can't tell my mom anything! She'd never let me."

"You see, Ted? It's too dangerous!" Nancy said.

Ted looked at the jaguar photo again, then said "Nancy's right, Martika. It *is* dangerous, there are risks. But I think you're my best hope of getting Jennifer back safely. I don't know how you do what you do with that psychic stuff . . . but you seem to have some connection to the jaguar and to my daughter. But if you don't want to do it, I understand. It's a lot for me to ask."

Martika felt all their eyes on her, waiting for an answer. She was scared of breaking into the Hayes house and even more worried about getting out. Maybe her powers weren't strong enough? But if she wasn't supposed to get involved, why was she having the dreams about Jennifer? And the psychometry episode with her bracelet? If the jaguar wasn't part of Martika's destiny, why was it coming up in so many areas of her life?

She remembered Tía Tellín's advice to trust her instinct. She closed her eyes and took a deep breath, listening for what it was saying to her. When she opened them she looked at Ted and said, "I'll do it."

The Ford Fiesta inched past the UCLA campus, caught in bumper-to-bumper traffic. From their silence, Martika knew that Lola and Ramón were uncomfortable with what had happened at Ted's house. She looked out the window at the Pauley Pavilion sports stadium.

"Are you excited about coming here in the fall?" Martika asked Ramón. He had won a scholarship to the highly competitive UC campus.

"Sure, it's going to be great as long as this old car holds up." He hesitated then asked, "How did you do that? With Ted's watch?"

"I don't know. I wasn't sure it would work, but I just did what Tía Tellín told me . . . and the images came," Martika replied.

"Could you do that with me? Or Lola?"

"I guess."

"Don't even *try* with me. It would freak me out!" Lola said.

"I'm the same person I've always been! It's the same as having a talent for soccer or playing the guitar," Martika said defensively.

Ramón laughed. "I play soccer and I can tell you this, what went down with Ted's watch is *nothing* like a bunch of guys kicking a ball around a field!"

Martika laughed with him and Lola joined in. "Are you going to put one of those neon signs in your window that says PSYCHIC? You could read people's cards and make bank!"

Martika reached into the backseat and gave Lola's thick black hair a yank.

"Ouch! That's not real—it's a piece, girl!" Lola protested, adjusting her hair. "I bought it at the swap meet. Don't mess it up!"

"And you really think you can help Ted with the statue? It's pretty risky," Ramón asked more seriously.

"I'm going to try," Martika said.

They drove in silence. Martika stared at the diagram of the Hayes house. Ted had drawn circles in red ink around the areas where the art collection was kept. She closed her eyes and tried to commit the layout to memory, to imagine herself inside the huge, mazelike house. She felt her stomach tighten. What had she gotten herself into?

Detective Guest made his way through the busy office of the Rampart Division Police Department. Uniformed officers and plainclothes detectives gathered at the coffee machine, waiting for the day's assignments. As Lieutenant Mike Robin passed by, Guest corralled him.

"Lieutenant, I'd like to get a warrant to search a building downtown. There may be a kidnapping victim inside."

Robin stopped and looked at him skeptically. "A kidnapping victim? How come this is the first I've heard of it?"

"It hasn't been reported yet, but I heard about it out on the street," Guest explained.

"Another one of your gang connections?"

After so many years on the force, Guest was known for having a cautious rapport with certain gang members. He knew he couldn't reveal that his source was a fifteen-year-old girl without looking like an idiot. And if he mentioned Ted's name, there would be the full-scale investigation that Blasi had warned against.

"Yeah, there's been some talk about a deal that went bad. You know, retribution," Guest covered.

"Look, John, I appreciate that you've got your ear to the ground, but I've got too many cases and not enough manpower. We just got word on a shooting in Inglewood, and I'm putting every available person on the home invasion homicides out in Santa Clarita. And someone just called in an Amber Alert. I can't spare anyone for a crime that hasn't even been reported, even if there's talk on the street. Maybe when things calm down, I'll consider it."

Before Guest could respond, Robin disappeared into his office, closing the door behind him.

Jennifer dug her fork into the McDonald's salad. For six days she hadn't eaten anything other than greasy fast food. When Javier showed up she was expecting another Quarter Pounder meal with large fries. She looked up at him watching her eat.

"Thanks. I was getting pretty sick of burgers and fries. I never thought I'd be so happy to see lettuce!" Jennifer said gratefully.

"No problem. I was wondering . . . if your mom is in New York, who takes care of your house and does the cleaning and all that?"

"Why do you assume that my mom would do that? She might be a brain surgeon and have no time for mopping floors," Jennifer said pointedly.

Javier smiled. "Sorry. I guess I'm more macho than I thought."

Jennifer swallowed a forkful of salad. "Well, my mom is not a brain surgeon, but she's never done any housework in her life. We have a housekeeper. Her name is Aurelia. She's been with us for years."

Javier didn't change his expression, careful not to give away his surprise.

Jennifer continued. "Does your mom work, or does she stay home and take care of the house?"

Javier replied, "She does both. She and my dad work on the maintenance crew at a couple of office buildings downtown. And when she's done, she comes home and cooks dinner for all of us and does the laundry."

"So she's got two full-time jobs. And one pays no salary," Jennifer said.

He had never thought of it that way. He was so accustomed to seeing other women in his neighborhood do the same thing, it seemed normal to him.

While Jennifer ate, Javier hunched deeper into his chair. He felt more and more uncomfortable keeping an eye on her for Mojito. He had been expecting a spoiled rich girl who whined all day. Instead, Jennifer was just like his sister, Lola, or Martika. She was somebody's daughter, somebody's friend. But in the gang, they taught him that everything was black and white and that people who weren't part of it didn't count.

"Do you have any brothers or sisters?" Javier asked.

"Nope. My parents could hardly handle one, let alone any more. You have a sister, right?"

"And a brother—his name is Ramón. He's a year older."

"Cool. You guys must be tight," Jennifer said.

"Not really. He's Mr. Perfect, you know? Everything he does is right. He's an athlete, the top student, popular."

"And you?" Jennifer asked.

"I'm just . . . you know, the brother. They just think of me as Ramón's brother."

Jennifer said nothing but she knew what he meant. She knew what it was like to feel like your own family looked right through you and didn't see who you really were.

Somewhere on Alameda Street, an MTA bus sounded its horn. Jennifer's plan had been to get Javier to see her sympathetically, as a real person, with feelings. And she had succeeded. But she hadn't counted on seeing him the same way.

Ramón pulled his Fiesta up in front of Tía Tellín's house, and Martika got out.

"So what do we do now?" Lola asked.

"I'm going to talk it over with Tía Tellín, and then I'll call you. I don't want you getting into any trouble."

"And we don't want you going into that big house without someone covering you. Ted seems like a cool guy, but you need your own crew to be with you," Ramón said.

"Your *gente*!" Lola shouted, high-fiving Martika through the open window as the car pulled away.

Martika saw Detective Guest's sedan parked in the driveway. Before she could knock, Tía Tellín opened the door and said, "You're late today."

"I need your advice, Tía."

They moved into the parlor, where Detective Guest was putting on his jacket, preparing to leave.

"Hello, Martika," he said. "Maybe you can convince your aunt to get a fax machine? I had to come all the way over here to drop off one piece of paper."

He picked it up from the coffee table. "This is the background check on Ted Colton. Seems the guy is into a few things besides selling cars. He has ties to the Russian mafia here in Los Angeles, probably related to money laundering. And from the look of his associates, it's likely he's involved in smuggling on the black market."

"I guess background checks are pretty accurate," Martika said. She told about her visit to Colton's house and how Ted and Nancy had caught them.

"Jennifer was kidnapped because Ted messed with the wrong guy over this statue." She took the jaguar photo from her backpack and handed it to them. When Tía Tellín looked at it, the color drained from her face. The old woman sank onto the sofa, her eyes glued to the photo.

"What's wrong, Tía?" Martika asked.

"Now it all makes sense," Tía Tellín said quietly. She held the photo out for Martika.

"This is the Jaguar of Uxmal. It is a powerful icon, stolen hundreds of years ago from the Temple of the Magician, at the sacred ruins of Uxmal in Yucatán. Our people have been seeking it for centuries. This is why you've been having these dreams and visions. It has been calling out to you. You must find it and return it to its rightful place."

A shiver ran up Martika's back. The Jaguar of Uxmal was the missing piece of the puzzle. It explained everything: the connection to Jennifer, the strange dreams, the tingling sensation, even her class project at school! But now her task was more complicated. Ted wanted the statue to free his daughter. Anything else that it represented wouldn't matter to him. Tía Tellín looked at Martika, her amber eyes steady. "The girl's father, he wants your help, doesn't he?"

"Yes.

"Does he know where the statue is now?" Detective Guest asked.

She told them about the deal that went bad with Eddie Blasi. At the mention of Blasi's name, Detective Guest's eyes lit up.

"Eddie Blasi? We'd love to get something concrete on him. The guy is mixed up in all kinds of dirty business, but he always manages to keep himself covered."

Martika was relieved. "Then the police can pick him up, can't they? Or they can go out to Hayes's house? The jaguar was on the black market and that's illegal, isn't it?"

Guest shook his head. "We can't just show up at someone's home to search it without probable cause, especially someone as prominent as R.J. Hayes. As for Blasi, same thing. Ted Colton hasn't filed a police report, so we can't just bring Blasi in for questioning, even if we know he's involved. He's slippery and savvy as well. He has one of the biggest lawyers in town on retainer."

Martika had hoped they could get the statue back without

her going into the Hayes house with Ted. She was having second thoughts about it, serious second thoughts. Detective Guest walked to the door.

"I can see myself out. And Martika? Have you had any more dreams about the place where they're holding Jennifer? I went looking around in the industrial section and saw a few buildings that might match what you described. I could use a few more details."

Martika shook her head. "Sorry, I haven't got anything new to add."

"Let me know if any new information . . . comes through. I'm trying to get a warrant to go into one of them but it doesn't look good, what with no police report. Keep me posted, okay? Good night, ladies." The heavy door closed behind him.

"What does Mr. Colton want you to do?" Tía Tellín asked.

"He wants me to go out there with him, to see if I can help him find the jaguar." Martika half hoped that Tía Tellín would discourage her but she sat quietly, thinking.

"What do you think I should do?" Martika asked finally.

"On one hand, you are a fifteen-year-old girl and you have no business breaking and entering private property."

Tía went to the bookcase, pulled down a volume, and continued. "But you are not an average fifteen-year-old girl. You are a *curandera*. And the Jaguar of Uxmal has called upon you to find it, which means helping Ted Colton. I know it is intimidating and you wish you had not been dragged into all of this, but remember: *No hay mal que por bien no venga.*"

There is no bad thing that doesn't bring some good with it.
Martika had heard her mother say it a million times.

Tía Tellín leafed through the pages of the book until she
found what she was looking for. She handed the open book to
Martika.

"Here it is. This is Uxmal. At one time it was the greatest
metropolitan and religious center in Yucatán. Its ruins still
stand today."

Martika looked at the drawings of the ancient ruins, elaborate structures rising out of the jungle, carved with flowers
and animal figures. Tía Tellín pointed to a drawing of a tall
pyramid with a square temple at the top.

"The Temple of the Magician was built by a powerful
shaman, a dwarf who challenged the king to a competition.
According to legend, he built the pyramid in one night with
his magic. Its doors and windows are designed to align with
the orbit of the planets. The western stairway faces the setting
sun of the summer solstice. The temple—"

Martika's gasp cut off her words. On the next page was an
ancient drawing of the jaguar statue. Its spots and markings
were the same as in the photo Ted had given her.

"That's it! That's the jaguar!"

Tía turned the page back to the drawing of the ruins. "And
that is the place it must be returned to, *mija.*"

"Do you think I'm powerful enough to help Ted find it?

I've just started to learn about my powers," Martika asked nervously.

"I wouldn't want you to go into this dangerous situation unprepared. Now that we know the task at hand, I will work with you."

"But how can I develop the kind of power I'm going to need? I have to do it in a few days. Maybe it shouldn't be me. It should be someone with experience."

Tía Tellín sat Martika down next to her and said solemnly, "One of the hardest parts of being a *curandera* is accepting the challenges that the universe gives you. It is not all the magic and mystery of having special powers. It is also a responsibility. You have a connection to the statue. It has been reaching out to you through your dreams and through Jennifer. It wants *you* to find it, Martika. *You* are the only one who can fulfill your destiny. If you were not powerful enough, it would not have chosen you. You must trust yourself and your abilities."

Martika considered Tía Tellín's words and then asked, "So where do we start? I need a *curandera* crash course."

Tía Tellín smiled as she stood and walked to the staircase, gesturing for Martika to follow.

"Fortunately, there is no such thing. We must help you to gather as much information as possible before you go out to the Hayes house. Since your power is showing itself in your dreams, you must learn how to enter the dreamtime at will. This is called conscious dreaming."

Conscious dreaming? Martika thought, following Tía Tellín. It seemed like a contradiction.

"I had another dream about the jaguar. I was chasing him down a beach," she said.

"Then back to the beach we shall go," Tía Tellín replied with certainty.

Fourteen

✾

In the spirit room, Martika lay on the rush mat, her eyes closed, listening to Tía Tellín's rhythmic voice as she hit the *tunkul* drum.

"For dream reentry, first you must be in a state of deep relaxation. Listen to your breathing, the beat of your heart. Next you must overcome the barrier of fear, the fear of moving to an altered state of consciousness. Let go of any anxiety you may have."

Martika followed Tía's instructions, breathing with the rhythm of her heart. Soon she could hear its steady beat in her head. Her limbs felt weightless.

I am not afraid . . .

Tía Tellín's voice sounded as if it came from far away, "Now you must have clarity of purpose. Why are you going back to the beach? What do you want from the jaguar?"

Martika felt her consciousness loosening its grip on the day's events, the present reality. She drifted.

Slowly she became aware of the breeze off the ocean. She smelled the salt in the air. Her feet sank into the warm sand. She was back on the beach. . . .

Tía Tellín's voice merged with the steady rhythm of the *tunkul* drum. "The jaguar wants to show you. He has led you to this place."

Martika saw his huge spotted form running down the beach. She followed until he turned to face her as he had in her dream. She felt a rush of fear. She could hear him breathing. She could see the pupils of his amber eyes. She asked him, Show me where you are. Lead me to the right place.

With a graceful toss of his head, he sauntered past her, brushing his shoulder against her hand. She felt the heat of his body. She smelled the pungent scent of his fur. She followed him, moving in a slow, rhythmic gait. Farther and farther down the beach the jaguar walked, looking back at her from time to time with his great, glowing eyes, making sure that she followed him. At the base of a tall cliff, the big cat stopped. Martika looked up at the huge white Hayes mansion. She knew that was her destination. The jaguar climbed the winding stone stairway—

Outside a car's brakes screeched. *CRASH!* Martika awoke out of her dream state. She sat up on her elbows, frustrated.

"I was on the beach! I saw the jaguar—I followed him to the base of the cliff, below the house. We started up the stairs and then that damn accident happened outside!"

Tía Tellín peered out the window. A crowd of neighbors had gathered around a smashed SUV.

"This is one of the difficulties for shamans who live in the city, *mija*. The modern world is always intruding. But you did good work today. We will continue this way until the Balam has shown you where to find him."

Martika could hardly contain her excitement. She had reentered the dreamtime at will, and the jaguar had communicated with her! Her head felt heavy and tired but she didn't care.

"I'll walk home with you," Tía Tellín said. "I'm visiting a friend on the other side of the park."

Martika saw her take her cards and herb bundles and knew that someone in the neighborhood had requested Tía Tellín's help.

They made their way down the hill and across the park, past the groups of young men playing soccer and families grilling sausages and sweet peppers on hibachis. The fresh smell of grass and the smoke from the grill mingled with the shouts of the *fútbolistas*. Someone turned up a boom box, and mariachi music wafted into the air. Martika took it all in, thinking it was just a regular soon-to-be-summer evening in

Echo Park. Except for one thing: the job ahead of her was anything but regular.

As she climbed the stairs to her apartment, Martika knew she would have to work hard to concentrate on her homework. After conscious dreaming, her World History essay was the last thing she wanted to think about. She stuck her key into the lock, but before she could turn it, her father yanked open the door.

"Where have you been?" he demanded.

Martika was caught off guard.

"Hi, Papi," she said, moving past him to the kitchen. Her mother was stirring a large pot of *chile verde*. Aurelia cast her a nervous glance but said nothing.

"*Dime!* Where were you?" her father asked, more insistently.

"I-I-I was out with Lola and Ramón," Martika stammered.

"*¡No me mientes!*" Camiso's shout echoed off the thin walls of the apartment.

"Your father saw the altar in your room, *mija*. I told him about taking you to see Tía Tellín and how you've been studying with her," Aurelia said, wiping her hands on her apron.

"You have no business going over there, learning all of that mumbo jumbo. You're not to go back there again! *¿Entendiste?*"

Martika knew she couldn't stop going to Tía Tellín's, not

now. "Papi, it's not mumbo jumbo. It's a gift, it's history. I'm learning all kinds of things from Tía Tellín—"

He interrupted her. "Whatever you're learning with her, you don't need to know. You do your learning at school."

"Papi, it's interesting and I'm learning how to control these gifts, how to use them in a good way."

Camiso lost his temper, pounding his palm for emphasis. "You know how hard your mother and I worked to come here so you could have a better life? So you could be a modern girl with modern opportunities and choices? I am not going to let my daughter get caught up in a bunch of old ways that I don't even understand!"

Martika was not accustomed to arguing with her father. Theirs was a traditional Latin family and her father's word was final. But she knew that this was not a regular disagreement about going to a party or breaking her curfew. Martika surprised herself when she said quietly, "Just because you don't understand it, Papi, doesn't mean it was right for you to keep it from me. I'm sorry if you don't want me to work with Tía Tellín anymore, but I won't stop. It's my gift and it's my choice."

Aurelia could see the anger flash in Camiso's eyes, and she tried to diffuse the tension. "Camiso, what harm can it do? She's not getting into any trouble—"

He cut her off with a dismissive wave of his hand. "*¡Cállate, mujer!* You've done enough damage!"

Martika felt something surge inside her. Maybe it was the stress and tension of the day. Maybe it was her own buried anger at her father for her parents' separation. Maybe it was the wounded look that she saw in her mother's eyes when Camiso ordered her to keep quiet that way. Martika had never raised her voice to her father until now. She snapped back at him. "Don't you talk to Mami that way! You can't come over here and order everyone around, Papi. You're the one who left!"

Her words hung in the air like smoke after a lightning strike. His eyes blazed with anger and embarrassment. He grabbed Martika by the arm. "I am the father. You are the daughter. You will do as I say!"

"I am more than just your daughter! I am a *curandera*!" Martika yelled back. On the stove, the flame under the pot of *chile verde* made a popping sound. It swept out, catching the corner of a kitchen towel. Aurelia quickly grabbed it, tossed it into the sink, and doused it with water.

"This damn stove, Camiso! I told you the pilot needs adjusting again. It could have burned the house down!"

Camiso answered defensively. "It was fine after the last time I fixed it." He leaned over the stove, removing the burner plates. Aurelia shooed him away.

"*Ya, ya basta.* You should go, *hombre*. It's been a long day and we're all worked up. See? You've upset *la nena*."

Martika hadn't moved; her eyes were fixed on the stove.

Camiso grabbed his jacket from the couch, his anger dissolving into regret. He looked at Martika and Aurelia apologetically.

"Bueno, me voy. I'll be by on Sunday." He closed the door behind him. Aurelia turned back to the stove.

"He didn't mean anything by all of that, *mija.* You know how your papi is . . . *¡qué machote!*"

Martika stood still, her eyes riveted to the flame that Aurelia had reignited. Martika knew it wasn't the pilot light that had malfunctioned. She had felt the power surge up through her whole body, in her palms, and behind her eyes just before the flame exploded and spread. It was Soraya's Fire.

Fifteen

❀

Jennifer slept restlessly under the cotton blanket. Javier's eyes felt heavy, even though he had just finished his third cup of coffee. It was early morning; the sun had not yet broken over the eastern horizon. Javier had lied to his parents and told them he was staying over at a friend's house in order to be the one on night watch. He was worried that Mojito might show up in the middle of the night. It was clear his *jefe* had developed some kind of fascination with Jennifer, and Javier was afraid of what could happen.

They had orders from Blasi not to hurt her in any way, but Mojito was too unpredictable and too drugged out to act normally. Javier knew that Kiko and the other young guys weren't going to stand up to Mojito if he lost control. When he heard a car pull up and Mojito whistling on his way up the stairs, Javier knew he was right to trust his instincts. He heard

Mojito shout, "¡*Güerita!* It's me! Time to get up!"

Javier looked at his watch. It read 4:45. He moved to the door, trying to be quiet.

"Hola, *jefe.* She's asleep," he whispered.

"Well, she's not asleep anymore, is she? Hey! ¡*Güera!* Wake up! It's time for breakfast!" Mojito shouted again.

Jennifer woke with a start. Mojito stood in the doorway. His eyes were red and swollen and he smelled of sweat and liquor.

"We get up early in this joint!" Mojito laughed a high-pitched giggle. He was wired and jumpy, obviously high on something. Javier and Jennifer looked cautiously at each other as Mojito opened the grocery bag and pulled out a large supermarket birthday cake, decorated with brightly colored icing.

"Today is my birthday, *güera*, and you and I are going to celebrate! What do you have for me?"

Jennifer looked to Javier, confused. "Do you mean a-a-a gift?" she stammered.

Mojito moved close to her, his eyes flat and deadly. His mood had shifted.

"You don't have no gift for me? Is that any way to treat me after all I've done for you? I brought you that bathroom stuff. I brought you clean clothes. I brought you food to eat and this is how you repay me?"

"I didn't know it was your birthday. I can't leave this room," she answered, frightened.

Mojito ran his greasy fingers over her blond hair, looping a thick strand around his hand and pulling her toward him.

"You sure you don't have anything to give me? I can think of a thing or two, *güerita*."

Jennifer met his bloodshot gaze, unable to hide her fear.

"Hey, come on, *jefe*! You want some of this cake? It looks real good. Do you mind if I have a piece?" Javier asked loudly, trying to get Mojito's attention.

Mojito released Jennifer and turned to him. "Go ahead. This is my birthday party. Your daddy still hasn't come up with the goods, *güerita linda*. The head honcho ain't happy. Something's gotta give, you know? Maybe you're just gonna stay here with me."

He shoveled a piece of cake, thick with frosting, into his mouth. Javier handed Jennifer a piece of cake on a paper towel. She took it reluctantly, trying to hide her dismay at Mojito's news.

"Go on, eat it," Mojito said.

"I'm not really hungry," she said.

Mojito shouted at her, his eyes furious, "EAT IT!"

She brought the cake to her mouth and took a bite. Mojito looked at both of them, grinning.

"Quite a party, huh?" he said. His laugh echoed off the walls of the abandoned building.

Martika stood in the middle of a steep and narrow stair-way. A yellow light cast a muted glow. There were voices above. Should she walk toward them? Or should she go down into the room below? She walked down several steps. The smell of earth and rock . . . a chill in the air . . . total darkness at the bottom. She descended and heard a low purring and chuffing from the shadows. The big cat was in the room below, somewhere in the depths of the house. She stepped into the room, her eyes adjusting to the darkness. Then she saw him, deep in the corner, in an alcove carved into the rock wall. The jaguar sat and preened, flashing his brilliant white teeth. He was waiting for her.

She approached him and he stepped out, his velvety paws silently padding on the stone floor. Suddenly she felt a rush of wind. The blackness closed in around her. She was in a tunnel, a narrow tunnel. The smell of the salt air, the damp breeze. She crawled toward it—she had to get there—but where did it lead?

The scene dissolved. . . .

Martika awoke. She did not know what to make of the dream. She had been studying the map of the Hayes estate. She knew the art collection was kept in the big open rooms at the south end of the house, not in a dark cellar. She knew she had to trust that the meaning of the dream would become clear. She had hoped for another dream about Jennifer; there hadn't been one in several days.

Maybe Blasi had hurt her? Or something worse?

Martika pulled the covers over her head and closed her eyes, willing away the thought. *Everything will work out*, she told herself in the early-morning darkness of her bedroom.

In the kitchen Aurelia had packed Martika's lunch in a small cooler, something she rarely did. It was leftovers of last night's *chile verde* with a salad and an oatmeal cookie.

"Morning, Mom. What's up with the lunch?" Martika asked, pleased.

"Just some leftovers to take to the library. I know how hard you're studying for finals, and how much time you're spending with Tía Tellín," Aurelia replied, peeling an apple. Her voice trailed off and Martika knew that there was something else coming. She poured her cereal and waited. Finally Aurelia said, "Your papi didn't mean to be so hard on you last night, Martika. He's just worried."

"About what? It's not like I'm missing school and hanging out with a bunch of gangbangers. Tía Tellín's got to be close to eighty. What kind of trouble am I going to get into with her?"

Aurelia moved to Martika, still holding the half-peeled apple. She saw Martika look at it questioningly and explained, "There are pesticides in the apple skin. I read about it yesterday while I was at the Kmart. About your papi, you're right. He doesn't understand these gifts you have. I don't understand it, either. All I know is that since you've been working with Tía

Tellín, you don't seem to be so nervous about those crazy dreams, right?"

Martika had considered telling her mother about the plans to help Ted find the jaguar and free Jennifer. But if her mother was so worried about the dangers in an apple peel, what would she do if she knew Martika was going to break into a big house in Malibu and steal an ancient relic?

Aurelia continued, "I know you're young and it's exciting to learn about these psychic things or whatever they are, but you're not going to let it get in the way of your studies, are you? You can't jeopardize all the hard work you've done up to now, *mija*. In a couple of years you'll be applying to college and you'll have to get a scholarship to go to a good school."

This had been drummed into her head since Martika had been a child and she took her first IQ test. She would be the one to go to college, she would get a good job, she would do all the things her parents had been unable to. And she wanted to do those things. More than anything Martika wanted to make her parents proud, to be able to make their lives easier when she was grown up. Her mother was right; she couldn't let her work with Tía Tellín and the mystery of finding the jaguar take too much of her time. What was she going to write on her college applications? "I am the head of the debate club and a member of student council. I am also a *curandera*, I have psychic dreams and I'm pretty sure I can start fires if I set my mind to it."

Aurelia was still talking. "So just have fun with it, okay? Go learn about your history or dreams or whatever Tía Tellín is teaching you. But just have a good time with it, okay? *No lo tomes muy en serio, mija.*" Don't take it too seriously, her mother said.

Too late for that, Martika thought.

Sixteen

❁

*M*artika scanned the park for Ramón and Lola but couldn't find them in the sea of families and Saturday soccer players. She went to the pay phone and dialed Ted's number.

"Hello?"

"It's Martika, Mr. Colton."

"Hey! What time and where?" Ted was coming to Echo Park with Mike DiCario to finalize the plans.

"How about four o'clock at Rodeo's Grill?"

"Great. Where is it?" he asked.

"Sunset at Echo Park Boulevard, a couple blocks east of Alvarado, the north side of the street."

"See you then! We'll have everything planned down to the last detail, don't worry. And Martika? Thank you again." Ted's voice sounded optimistic. Martika hoped she wouldn't let him down. She dialed Ramón's cell phone.

"What's up?" he answered. She could hear the sounds of kids shouting and laughing in the background.

"Rodeo's Grill, four o'clock," she said. He passed the information on to Lola, who groaned loudly before wresting Ramón's phone from him.

"Rodeo's Grill? Isn't that kind of low-end for Ted? Why didn't you choose The Brite Spot? They just got new booths," she said.

"I had a few other things on my mind," Martika replied.

"Yeah, I guess. Like not getting caught by the security guys or eaten by the guard dogs, huh?" Lola said.

"Well, that makes me feel better, Lola! See you at four," Martika hung up with an anxious laugh. Lola was right; those were the exact things she had on her mind.

Camiso knocked on the door to the apartment. He held a small stuffed bear wearing a Dodgers cap. He knew Martika was too old for toys but he had bought it on impulse, wanting to give her something to make up for their argument. Aurelia opened the door.

"*¿Qué haces aquí, viejo? Adelante,*" she said, surprised.

"Is Martika home from school yet?" he asked, stepping inside.

"No. She stayed late to use the computer lab."

"Do you think she might be . . . over there?" He gestured toward Tía Tellín's house.

Aurelia rolled her eyes at him.

"And what if she is? What then?" she asked. Camiso shrugged, knowing that there was no way he could stop Martika from doing something she was determined to do.

"I guess this day was going to come sooner or later," he said.

"She's right. It's her gift. She has a right to learn how to use it."

"She's become so independent," he said wistfully.

"And isn't that what we wanted? For her to be an independent girl with her own ideas? We can't expect her to be that way only with other people and not with us."

Camiso knew Aurelia was right. She always asked the hard questions and was willing to face the answers, whatever they might be. He respected that quality, but sometimes it drove him crazy. He set the stuffed bear on the sofa arm.

"Will you give this to her when she gets back?"

Aurelia picked it up with a smile. "I'm sure she'll like it."

"I didn't mean to get so angry last night. I think I was too hard on her," he said sheepishly.

"Only on her?" Aurelia asked.

Camiso felt his face flush, then he added, "I didn't mean to be rude. I had no business talking to you that way."

Aurelia smiled briefly at his apology and said, *"Gracias, Camiso."*

Before the separation she would have accepted his outburst

and never pushed for an apology, but now things had changed. Martika was right. He couldn't come around here telling people what to do, even if he was still her husband. Not when he had left for another woman.

She could sense that he was hoping for an invitation to sit and talk, but she went to the kitchen to start dinner. If he wanted a woman to make coffee and listen to his complaints about work, let him go home to his young *pollita*, Josefina, who couldn't cook or keep a clean house from what Aurelia heard. Camiso stood for a moment, feeling very out of place.

"*Bueno, me voy*. Have Martika call me, okay?" he asked awkwardly.

"Of course. *¡Hasta el domingo!*" Aurelia said with a casual wave. She smiled to herself as the door closed.

Javier thumbed through a magazine, keeping one eye on Jennifer, who had been quiet and withdrawn all day.

"You hungry?" he asked.

"No thanks," she answered. She had been depressed since Mojito's visit. Her father hadn't come up with the ransom, and Mojito planned to keep her with him. She couldn't bear to think about it. Jennifer turned to face the wall.

"What's wrong?" Javier asked.

She didn't look at him. "What do you think is wrong? I'm being held here against my will with a crazy person calling the shots."

Jennifer leaned her forehead against the wall, and Javier could see that she was about to cry. He moved his folding chair closer to her.

"I know Mojito can be kind of crazy. He gets really worked up—"

"*Kind of* crazy? I'd say being a crank freak makes you more than *kind of* crazy."

"How do you know he's using crank?" Javier asked. He knew Mojito was hooked on the drug, the *veteranos* in the park had told him.

Jennifer laughed sarcastically. "You think kids aren't using crank in Pacific Palisades? I know kids who've gotten hooked on everything from coke to heroin. Methamphetamine, barbiturates, Valium, Vicodin. You name it, they can get it. Usually from their parents' medicine chest."

Javier was silent. In his neighborhood a lot of people got into drug trouble; he was used to it. But he couldn't imagine what it would be like if his own parents did drugs.

"Do your folks do drugs?" he asked tentatively.

Jennifer thought for a moment, then she replied, "Well, my mother is an alcoholic. I wish I could say she's recovering, but that would be a lie. And my dad? He's a good-time guy. He's up for whatever is being passed around. He may not do drugs in front of me, but when I'm up in my room or at a party? Sure. On top of it, he can't sleep without Ambien and he needs Adivan for his nerves. I'm sure he's tried ecstasy with those bimbos he goes out with. . . . So yeah, I'd have to say yes to your question. And you?"

"I've smoked weed a few times but I haven't tried anything heavy. And I know my brother and sister haven't. I'd kick Lola's ass if she got into that crap."

"Why are you in a gang?" Jennifer asked suddenly. "I don't get that. You're so smart. How did you get mixed up with a freak like Mojito?"

Javier blushed at the compliment. He was so used to hearing that Ramón was the smart one; he didn't know how to respond.

"I don't know. I get mad seeing how hard everything is. The way the cops are always jacking people in my neighborhood for no reason. It's like you can never get ahead. With the gang, I feel like someone. My homies and I are respected on the street. And a lot of them are good guys."

She said quietly, "You can see how insane this is, can't you? Keeping me here this way?"

Javier looked down at his shoes. "Yeah, I know," he replied.

"Please, will you help me get out of here?"

Javier could hear her desperation. But he couldn't break the trust Mojito and the others had put in him, letting him join the gang, giving him a place to belong. Not for this girl he didn't even know, who lived in a world so different from his. He didn't know what to say to her. So he said nothing.

❈　❈ · ❈

"I told you never to try it! Soraya's Fire is a powerful gift, too powerful for you. It is not a game!" Tía Tellín's voice was tight and furious. Martika had just told her about the stove incident.

"I didn't do it on purpose. It happened when I got angry," Martika protested.

Tía Tellín reminded herself that Martika was still a novice. She took a deep breath and said more calmly, "Then anger is something you must be careful with. Some gifts are like that; they work spontaneously when you are in a state of extreme emotion. They are most dangerous and unpredictable. Anger can be positive. It can protect you and it can prompt you to take action. But it has a dark side as well. It can turn in on you and consume your life and your hope. What happened last night was a warning. You must be *very* careful."

Soraya's Fire was not something Tía Tellín had planned for. If Martika's parents had allowed her to grow up honoring and learning about her gifts, she would have the proper respect for Soraya's Fire. Martika was a typical modern girl, filled with curiosity and daring, feeling the invincibility of youth. Those qualities combined with Soraya's inheritance could prove to be very dangerous.

Ramón and Lola were waiting in front of Rodeo's Grill when Martika and Tía Tellín arrived.

"Mr. Colton and the private investigator are inside eating," said Lola.

"They're eating *here*?" Martika asked in disbelief.

Lola shrugged as they went inside. "*You* chose this dive . . ."

At a back table, Ted sat with DiCario, eating a plate of enchiladas. He waved his fork when he saw Martika.

"The food here is great! There's something I want to try on the menu. What's a *chicharrón*?" he asked.

Martika, Lola, and Ramón looked at one another, unsure how to describe the fatty, gelatinous skin of the pig. Tía Tellín introduced herself and asked diplomatically, "How is your cholesterol, Mr. Colton?"

"Not great," replied Ted.

Tía Tellín patted his hand. "Then you don't need to be eating any *chicharrón*."

A waitress cleared the plates and Ted laid out his map of the Hayes estate. With a red marker Ted outlined their path into the house.

"The trainer will take the dogs for their weekly exercise and training session in the afternoon. Once they are off the property and the security crew is distracted, we'll move in through the gates on the ocean side."

"You mean that Martika will go in with you?" Tía Tellín asked.

"Yes. I think that's the only way to use her . . . abilities. Don't you think?"

"And how will you guarantee her safety, Mr. Colton?"

Ted cleared his throat. "I will be with her every step of the way. I'll be carrying a firearm for protection. My team will be outside, ready to storm the property if anything goes wrong or if she is in any danger at any moment. We'll be communicating with wireless headsets. Everyone will know where everyone else is at all times."

DiCario spoke up. "I was with Chicago SWAT for ten years, ma'am, and I've assembled a crack team for this job. Ted explained your niece's abilities. All she has to do is point us in the right direction. We'll do the rest."

Ramón added, "And we'll be waiting just down the road. If she isn't out in thirty minutes, we're calling the police. No offense, Mr. Colton, but we have to back up Martika."

Ted nodded and continued, "It should take us fifteen minutes to get inside, find the jaguar, and leave. Martika will be on her way home before half an hour is up, I promise."

Tía Tellín said, "Your plan is very ambitious, Mr. Colton. Martika is my apprentice. She is just learning how to use her gifts. But I am confident that if the jaguar is there, she will be the one to find it."

Martika looked at her, wishing that she could feel the same certainty.

Detective Guest stopped at Alex Donuts in Hollywood; he had about an hour to kill before interviewing a robbery suspect. That would give him time to head downtown and take another look at those brick buildings in the industrial section.

Something about them bothered him, especially the fresh tire tracks in the parking lot. With the broken windows on the first floor, it wouldn't be hard to get inside to hide someone. Or to take a look around. Lieutenant Robin hadn't budged on the warrant, so Guest knew he had to take matters into his own hands. He had just pulled onto Franklin Avenue when his cell phone rang.

"Guest, what's up?"

He listened for a moment, then smacked the steering wheel in frustration. His robbery suspect had been shot in a drive-by. Guest hung a U-turn and headed back to the station. Looking for Jennifer would have to wait until later. He hoped he'd have the chance because he knew she was running out of time.

Seventeen

✿

*T*ed and DiCario drove down Sunset Boulevard toward the freeway without talking. Ted was deep in thought, going over the next day's plan. After a few blocks, he reached for his cell phone and dialed Eddie Blasi.

"Hello?" a voice answered.

"This is Ted Colton. I'm calling for Mr. Blasi." After a long wait Blasi came on the line.

"What news do you have for me, Ted?"

"Tomorrow I'll have the statue. I want to arrange the trade to get my daughter back."

There was a longer pause before Blasi responded.

"Tomorrow doesn't exist yet, Ted. Call me when you have the statue in your hands. You don't have much time left." Blasi hung up. Furious, Ted flipped his phone closed and pulled onto the freeway. DiCario asked, "You think that might have been a little premature? What if it doesn't work out tomorrow?"

"It will work out. It *has* to," Ted said with finality, never taking his eyes from the road.

Mojito pulled up to the garage at Eddie Blasi's condominium and gave his name to the security guard. He was in a foul mood. Blasi said the trade would take place tomorrow. Mojito would hand over Jennifer and collect the ransom. He had gotten used to that pretty blond *güerita*. He liked the idea of having her around, completely under his control. He'd never had a girl like her and he wasn't happy about turning her over to anyone, no matter what Blasi said.

He stepped into the elevator. *Eddie Blasi is a* pendejo *who doesn't have any idea how tough it is on the street. He lives up here like a king, making other people handle his dirty business for him,* Mojito thought, watching the elevator numbers climb to the penthouse.

He walked down the hallway and knocked on Blasi's door. Tavo opened it, nodding and ushering him in. Mojito looked around at the expensive décor: leather couches, thick Persian rugs, and exotic artifacts on the walls.

This guy who has it all is going to tell me to hand over my girl!

Blasi entered. "Hello, Mojito. Did Tavo offer you anything?"

Mojito shook his head. "No, I'm okay."

"You don't want a beer or a drink or anything? I have a full bar." Blasi gestured to the liquor cabinet casually. Mojito's eyes narrowed as he looked at Blasi's rail-thin form.

I could take him out with my bare hands.

Blasi lit a Gitanes cigarette and took a long drag on it. "Here's the deal. Colton guarantees he'll have the ransom tomorrow but I don't count on anything until it's done. In the event that he is correct, we make the trade tomorrow evening, late. You bring the girl and collect. I arrange the place. Easy trade, no complications."

Mojito felt his shoulder blades tighten. "What if the guy doesn't have it?"

"Then you take him out for wasting my time and energy," Blasi replied.

"And the girl?"

"If there's no statue, I don't care what happens to her as long as she's not walking around talking about anything, you understand?"

Mojito nodded. He understood perfectly.

Tía Tellín placed a thin leather cord around Martika's neck. Three blue-green jade stones hung from it, perfectly round and smooth. The lights in the spirit room were dim; the air smelled bitter and sweet from the herbs burning on the altar.

"These are powerful stones of protection, Martika. They were mined from the Puuc Hills by your ancestors. Many *curanderas* have worn them over the years when facing a difficult task."

Tía Tellín lit a bundle of herbs, waving it around Martika, wrapping her in its thick smoke.

"Sacred herbs to protect you and guide you." Then Tía Tellín spoke in a dialect that Martika did not understand.

> *"Ah uayom chichob, ah uayom tunob,*
>   *ah ziniltunob*
> *Ah uayom balamob-ox uayohob*
> *Can bak hab u xul u cuxtalob*
> *Tumen yohelob u ppiz kinob tubaob. . . ."*

When she had finished, Martika asked, "How are you going to keep the jaguar away from Blasi, Tía? Ted is handing it over as soon as possible to get Jennifer back."

"*No te preocupes, mija.* Leave that to me. You have a big enough job before you," Tía Tellín said.

Martika didn't know how her aunt was going to pull it off. Ted's associates were dangerous and desperate men, capable of anything. How was an eighty-something woman, barely five feet tall, going to thwart their plans for the jaguar?

At the door Tía Tellín took Martika by the shoulders and looked her in the eye. "Everything will work out just the way it is supposed to. You were called, Martika, you are powerful enough. Believe in yourself tomorrow and trust your instincts."

Martika nodded and Tía Tellín kissed her on the forehead.

"Thank you for helping me, Tía," Martika said.

"I'll be here waiting for word from you. Do not remove your amulet or your jade beads!" Tía Tellín called out as Martika walked through the gate. Tía Tellín stood at the front door looking after Martika until she became a small speck, crossing the park, her black ponytail swinging in rhythm with her step. Tía Tellín closed the door, picked up the phone, and dialed. "Detective John Guest, please."

Aurelia knocked quietly on the door to her daughter's room. Martika had hardly touched her dinner and had seemed distracted all evening. Aurelia found Martika at her desk, reading the large volume that Tía Tellín had given her.

"Hey, did you see the gift that Papi left?" Martika smiled at the stuffed bear.

"It's cute. I guess he thinks I'm still a little girl," Martika said.

"*Mija*, there is never going to be a day when you are anything other than your papi's little girl. Even when you're an old *ruca* like me."

Martika tossed the bear at Aurelia. *Ruca* was the same as calling someone an old bag; her mother was anything but. "You look better now than when you got married, Mami," she said.

Aurelia whistled in disbelief. "The day thirty-six looks better than eighteen, the devil will be lacing up his ice skates!"

Martika stood and pulled Aurelia in front of the mirror.

"No, really, Mami. When you were eighteen you were so pretty but you looked, I don't know . . . like a blank piece of paper. All the things that make you who you are weren't there yet. Does that make sense?"

Aurelia nodded and they stared at their reflections in the mirror, side by side. Martika looked just like her mother without the ample bosom or the curvaceous hips that came after childbirth. And without the years of worry at every trial and joy at every milestone that had been part of raising a daughter for fifteen years.

Martika wished she could tell her mother everything, about helping Ted and trying to get Jennifer back. Keeping it a secret made her feel bad, like she was breaking Aurelia's trust in her. And she would have liked to hear her mom say it would all be okay in the end.

Martika could sense tears coming on, and she gave her mother a hug to hide her face. Aurelia felt the tension in Martika's thin shoulders and asked quietly, "What's wrong, *mija?*"

Without breaking away, Martika whispered, "Nothing, Mami. I just love you."

Eighteen

✾

*M*ojito took another shot of tequila, waiting for his *gabacho* friend Keith to lay out some more crank. Mojito had just made a drug drop and gotten a nice chunk of cash. Now they were in Keith's garage apartment, kicking it, listening to Molotov. Keith snorted up a line of crank and passed the straw to Mojito. As the familiar rush kicked in, Mojito thought of Jennifer and the plan to turn her over tomorrow. *No way. He had his own plan.*

Even if her father showed up with the ransom, it would be easy to spin it so Blasi would think he'd been conned; just say the old man stiffed him, stash the statue. Blasi would never imagine that Mojito had the *cojones* to try something like that. Mojito would get rid of Colton and the girl would be his. Maybe cross the border, have a little holiday, and then he could make some cash on a pretty *güerita* like that. He knew the places to take her to, the ones that the local cops didn't bother as long as they got their cut. Screw Blasi and his rules about an easy trade, no complications. Tonight he was going to complicate things a little. Tonight he would have some fun with *la güerita esa*.

The moon shone through the bars of the window. The night air was strangely humid for Los Angeles; a summer storm was coming. Jennifer couldn't believe what Javier had just told her. Tomorrow, after her father delivered the ransom to Mojito, she would be released.

"Are you sure? It's not some crazy mind game?" she asked.

Javier shook his head. "No. I spoke to Kiko. He said Mojito had just come from Blasi's and he was waiting to get the information on when and where."

She would be free! Her father had come through, and she would get to go home! She could hardly contain her excitement but Javier seemed troubled.

"What's wrong?" she asked.

Javier hesitated. He didn't want to bring her down, but he had seen Mojito a few hours earlier, completely jacked up. He knew his *jefe* was angry and frustrated about giving up Jennifer. Javier didn't know why, but he just had a bad feeling about the whole thing. He attempted a smile and said, "I'm happy for you. I'm glad nothing got out of hand and you didn't get hurt or anything."

"Me too. Thanks for being there for me at Mojito's birthday party. That was pretty freaky."

Javier laughed. "What the hell was that about?"

Their laughter ended abruptly when they heard the sound of Mojito's car pulling into the vacant lot outside. Javier climbed to the window and watched him. He could tell Mojito was loaded. Javier took Jennifer by the arm and led her to the hallway.

"Come with me," he said.

"What's going on?" she asked, frightened.

"It's Mojito and he looks all messed up. I'm moving you to another floor." Javier pushed open the door to a dirty stairwell.

"Follow me. And walk quietly," he said.

"Why are we moving?" she asked.

"I saw him earlier," Javier said, "and I could tell he was all worked up about you. I'm afraid he might try and . . . do something, you know?" He chose his words carefully.

Jennifer knew perfectly well what he meant. She had felt the threat of it each time Mojito had tried to get close to her.

Javier continued. "I checked out some of the other floors to find a safe spot in case he flipped out. There's a storage closet on the tenth floor."

He took the stairs two at a time, trying to gauge where Mojito was in the building. They stopped to hear his heavy footfalls as he climbed the stairway below them. Javier grabbed Jennifer's hand and whispered, "Don't make any noise."

"Aren't you going to get in a lot of trouble?" Jennifer asked.

"Probably," he replied as they pushed open the door to the hallway of the tenth floor.

Javier led her to a dark closet that smelled of rodent droppings and chemicals. They waited in silence for Mojito to discover she was gone. A moment later, they heard the loud crash of something being knocked over.

"*¿¡QUÉ CHINGADA!?* Where is she?" Mojito bellowed, stomping down the hallway. He was in a frenzy. Javier and Jennifer didn't move, terrified.

After a beat Javier's cell phone rang, startling both of them. Could Mojito hear it? Javier switched it to vibration mode and let it ring again before he answered it.

"Hello?" Javier said.

"Where the hell is she? And where are you?" Mojito's voice was so loud that Jennifer could hear him clearly.

"*Jefe*, I'm glad you called. I've got the girl with me," Javier said.

"I gave you instructions not to leave for *any* reason!" Mojito shouted.

"Some people came around, *jefe*. They were looking in the parking lot and trying to get in the door," he improvised.

"Did they look like cops?" Mojito asked.

"I couldn't tell. I didn't want to risk being seen. But I thought they might come back, so I took the girl. I have my brother's car and we're driving around. I was just about to call you."

Mojito took a deep breath. The *güerita* was still under his control.

"Where are you?" Mojito asked.

"I don't know. I just got on the freeway. I think I'm out by Pomona. . . ," Javier lied.

Mojito calmed down. *Javier did good, keeping the girl away from any visitors. It would be just like that father of hers to try and pull off some eleventh-hour rescue.*

"Okay, keep driving with her. Don't stop anyplace where she can be seen or get away from you. Have her back here in a few hours. I'm waiting to hear from Blasi. And Javi? You did good, *mijo*, real good. You're my man," Mojito said.

Javier hung up and gestured for Jennifer to be quiet until they heard Mojito leave the building and drive off. Shaken, they sat in the dark, not speaking, for a long time afterward.

It was well past midnight but Tía Tellín's spirit room was alive with energy. A faint hum filled the air, as if a current of electricity were running through it. All the candles on the altar were lit, illuminating the faded photos and *santitos*. Fresh-cut herbs lay before the statues of Ixchel, the moon goddess; Kinich Ahau, the sun god; and Balam-Agab, the jaguar god of the night. In the center of the room, Tía Tellín sat in a circle marked by statues of the Bacabs, the Mayan deities who hold up the four corners of the sky. In front of her, sweet, acrid smoke rose from an *incensario* shaped like a bird. She wore a traditional Mayan *huipil*, embroidered with flowers. Her gray hair was long and loose, falling over her shoulders. She rocked back and forth, her eyes closed, deep in a trance.

The humming grew louder. The animal masks looked alive in the flickering candlelight. Slowly the drums hanging on the walls began to beat. A steady rhythm filled the room. The bone raspers and the *chaskas* started to shake. Now the humming became distinct; it was many voices whispering. The sounds mingled together, building to a crescendo, and suddenly Tía Tellín's eyes flew open, the amber irises glowing, her pupils dilated. She spread her arms out wide and turned her face up toward the sky. A flash of amber light filled the room and the drumming stopped. The humming of the voices died down. And where Tía Tellín had been sitting, a black crow pecked at the *incensano*, which had suddenly burned out.

Outside, a thunderclap announced that the storm had arrived. A gust of wind blew open the casement window. The crow flew to the windowsill and turned to cast a look back into the spirit room. Its eyes glowed amber in the moonlight. The crow spread its wings and disappeared into the night.

Nineteen

❀

The same abandoned room with the barred windows . . . the door opened and she was led out into a dirty hallway, down several flights of stairs, into a car. The engine sounded like thunder when it turned over. She was in the backseat, her hands bound. Where was she going? The car drove through deserted streets. All she could make out was the shadowy form of the driver, but there was danger . . . serious danger. Now the car was on a winding road, lights visible in the distance. The road twisted and turned, rising higher and higher above the city. Where was she being taken? Something was wrong, very wrong.

Martika sat up in bed. It was her first dream about Jennifer in days. Where was she being taken? If Tía Tellín was correct about the dreams, then at least Jennifer was still alive.

At breakfast Martika did her best to appear relaxed as her mother prepared to leave for work. Luckily Aurelia had a client in Pasadena that would take all day, and Camiso had to repair a retaining wall that had suddenly fallen in Studio City. Martika, Lola, and Ramón would meet at Ted's house at ten A.M. to follow him out to Point Dume. The passing storm had blown out the smog, leaving the sky clear and sunny.

"What time will you and Lola be back from the library?" Aurelia asked.

"We're going to go browse the shops on Sunset and Alvarado afterward, so . . . maybe around five?"

"Take your time, *mija*. I know you have a lot of studying to do." Aurelia kissed Martika and headed out the door. An hour later, the Ford Fiesta was hurtling down the 101 Freeway en route to Ted's house.

Forty minutes later, they pulled into the driveway on Amalfi Drive to find DiCario and his crew of guys driving away in a black Expedition with tinted windows. Ted loaded a large wicker basket into the trunk of his Mercedes; the car sat waiting with the motor running. Ted jumped in and drove out when he saw the Fiesta and signaled them to follow. Ramón stayed close on Ted's tail, taking the banked curves down to Pacific Coast Highway, the Fiesta's engine struggling to keep up with the Benz Turbo. Luckily PCH was clear of traffic, and they made a straight shot out to Malibu.

At the Point Dume Estates, the guard at the gate stopped them after Ted had driven through.

"Where're you kids going?" he asked, eyeing the beat-up Fiesta suspiciously.

"For a picnic," Martika replied.

"Who're you meeting in the Estates?" the guard pressed her. Martika saw Ted's car disappearing down the street. She leaned over Ramón and honked the horn loudly to get Ted's attention.

"My dad—you just let him through!" Martika said, annoyed.

Ted's car stopped and backed up to the gate. He got out and asked, "Is there a problem?"

Before the guard could respond Martika leaned out the window and said in her best bratty voice, "He won't let us in, Dad! I told him we were having a picnic!"

The guard raised the gate arm quickly, apologizing. "I'm sorry, sir. I didn't realize these kids were with you. Go on through."

Ted flashed him a smile. "Thank you. It's my daughter's birthday."

They drove along the winding streets to the trailhead of the hiking path. Ted took the basket from the trunk as the teens piled out of the Fiesta. It held wireless headsets and walkie-talkies.

"Quick thinking on the picnic idea, Martika!" Ted said, impressed.

"Thanks, *Dad*," she replied with a smile.

They followed the path past wild sage, Indian paintbrush, and scattered bursts of California poppy. The streets were quiet except for a few joggers. A black crow rooted among the wildflowers, searching for food.

They climbed out to the corner of the point and reached a rock promontory where they were not visible from the road. Ted unpacked the headsets and handed them out.

"Everyone check your headset. Make sure it works and you can hear clearly," he said. Martika slipped on her headset and adjusted the mouthpiece. She could hear all the members of the team checking in. DiCario and his crew were already staked out around the property. Ted took a pair of binoculars and fixed them on the Hayes estate. He saw the housekeepers in their starched white uniforms carry several large trash bags out to the garbage area. He checked his watch.

"They must be doing the kitchen. After this, they should go to the north corridor to clean the bedrooms," he said. The housekeepers disappeared back into the house.

"Want to look?" Ted handed the binoculars to Martika.

She brought them to her eyes and adjusted the blurry image until the Hayes estate was crystal clear. She could see the details of the window boxes that hung from the second-floor balconies, the bright red geraniums and yellow daisies. She closed her eyes and cleared her mind.

The jaguar is somewhere in there . . . all I have to do is find it. I will find it.

With a caw, the crow flew off, unnoticed. A moment later DiCario's voice crackled over the headsets.

"The animal trainer arrived to take the dogs for their workout. They should be leaving through the northeast gate to head down to the beach. And the gardener is moving to the west gate on the ocean side."

The gardener's small truck pulled up, and he opened the west gates of the property to begin clearing brush from the hillside.

"Gates are open. Time to make our move," Ted said.

Lola and Ramón came over to Martika.

"We'll be here waiting. If you get in trouble just yell '¡venga!' and we'll come running," Lola said.

"And we'll call the cops if you're not out within half an hour," Ramón added. He handed her his Swiss Army knife. "It's not much, but I always feel better when I have it." Martika slipped it into her pocket.

"You can hear me on the headset, right?" she asked.

Ramón smiled. "Loud and clear."

Martika and Ted walked down the bluff to the beach below. They crossed the sand without talking, both intent on the task ahead. They climbed the stairway that led to the edge of the Hayes property. As they crouched near the top, Ted checked his firearm. Martika looked away, nervous at being so close to a loaded gun. He handed her a white envelope.

"This is the money that Hayes paid for the jaguar. Leave it in the house when we take the statue," he said.

Martika pocketed the envelope and peered over the top step with Ted. A lone security guard patrolled the back of the house. He made a loop and headed around to the front. The gardener took a large bin of scrub brush and disappeared, leaving the gates open.

"It's a good thing Mr. Hayes is into saving the environment. The compost pile is at the far end of the lot," Ted chuckled.

Over the headset, DiCario's voice came through. "You're in luck. The guard on your side has just made it to the front, and he's stopping for a smoke with the guys over here. We don't have to do anything. He should be here for a couple of minutes, long enough to get into the house. Let me know when you're inside."

"Okay. We're going in," Ted said.

As Ted scrambled up the stone staircase, a piece of the top step broke off. He lost his footing and slid down the hillside. Martika tried to reach him, but she knew her own foothold was too precarious to risk throwing herself off balance.

"Are you okay?" she whispered.

He nodded but when he righted himself, his headset was gone, lost in the dense brush. They moved to the French doors. Closed.

"The kitchen doors are locked!" Martika whispered into the headset.

"Try the dog door—it should be open. Where's Ted?"

"He lost his headset in a fall."

"Jesus," DiCario muttered.

Martika motioned Ted toward the large dog door. She climbed through first and then heard a man's voice outside shout, "Stop right there or I'll drop you!"

She froze, waiting for someone to come through the dog door after her, but all she heard was the sound of a scuffle and Ted being led away. Then nothing. She was in the house alone. She looked around. She was in the laundry room.

"They caught Ted!" she whispered into her headset, panicked. "I'm in here by myself!"

"You're by yourself? Get out of there, girl!" Lola's frightened voice answered back.

"She's right, Martika! Get out now!" Ramón agreed.

DiCario's voice came over the headset, calm and reassuring.

"Don't worry. We're hidden right outside the front gate, and it's probably best for them to be distracted by Ted. You just do whatever it is that you do and find that statue. Leave the rest to us," he said.

Martika closed her eyes and cleared her thoughts, visualizing the layout of the house that she had studied so diligently in the past two days. She felt for the amulet and the jade beads around her neck. The steady hum of the appliances combined with the warm scent of clean laundry and bleach. She pictured the jaguar as she had seen him on the beach.

Where are you? I'm here. I've come, like you wanted. Show me where you are.

She felt the faint tingling at the base of her skull.

That's it. I'm here for you, Balam-Agab. Lead the way. . . .

Now the slight whispering of voices in her mind. He was answering her call. She stepped gingerly out into the hallway, determined to follow his voice.

Twenty

❀

$\mathcal{J}$ennifer had not slept all night; she and Javier had returned to the holding room in the early hours of the morning. They had talked until sunrise. Even though he had been involved in her kidnapping, Jennifer found she couldn't hold it against him. He had his reasons for being in Mojito's gang, and she knew she was in no position to judge them. And Javier had been a good friend to her, watching her back from the beginning.

It was late morning when they heard Mojito's engine roaring outside. A few minutes later he came through the door looking worn out and grungy.

"So I hear you went on a little trip last night, *güera*? With my homeboy?" He shook Javier's hand and wrapped an arm around his neck.

Jennifer kept her eyes averted and answered quietly, "Yes."

"And I bet you're all excited about going back to your rich daddy, aren't you?"

"What time will it be?" she asked.

"No idea, baby. But when I come by, be ready. We're going to take a ride, you and me."

Javier asked, "Do you want me to come with you, *jefe*? In case they try anything?"

Mojito shot him a quick glance, as hard as stone.

"No way, *mijo*. This is my show."

Ted took another punch to the gut but stayed on his feet. All of Hayes's security team had turned out to rough him up in the privacy of the five-car garage. The leader of the group was a heavily tattooed man named Buzz with a haircut to match. His massive fist connected with Ted's cheek, splitting it open with a spurt of blood.

"What did you think you were going to get?" he barked. Ted was seeing double, but he had to prolong this encounter to provide cover for Martika.

"I was hiking, man. I just saw the gates open and figured there was probably some good stuff inside."

Another punch.

Good thing I lost my headset. They don't need to know there's a team of us, Ted thought.

Buzz leaned in close, saliva flying. "You thought some

small-time crook like you was going to get past this crew? We're pros, man!"

Some professionals. A fifteen-year-old girl is in the house right now, taking your boss's precious statue.

For all of his bravado, Buzz was unnerved by the near miss. The guy had almost made it inside. Buzz turned to the others. "You guys give him what he deserves, I'm going to check the house, make sure nothing is missing."

Ted did his best to hide his panic as the group moved in on him. He knew Martika must still be inside, alone.

Martika crept down the south corridor of the enormous house as quietly as possible. In the distance she could hear the sound of a vacuum running. The rooms were large and open, flowing into one another seamlessly. She knew the art collection was in one of the gallery rooms on the southeast side of the house.

She passed the den and the huge formal dining room set for thirty with polished crystal and china. It looked as if the president were coming to dinner. The low vibration of the tingling grew stronger. She knew she was getting closer to the jaguar.

Just another fifteen yards or so . . .

The corridor seemed endless. Over the sound of the vacuum she thought she heard an outside door open and close. She stopped and listened, hovering outside a weathered rustic door with an iron bolt across it. Did she hear footsteps? The tingling was more intense now. *Better to keep moving...*

She hurried toward the end of the corridor and ducked down a short hallway that had to lead to the art gallery. She saw the heavy glass doors ahead of her, just where Ted said they would be. She pushed them open, silently praying she wouldn't set off the alarm.

She felt the hermetic seal give way and stepped into the stillness of a room filled with ancient carvings and statues. They were set on pedestals covered with natural muslin. She couldn't see the jaguar anywhere. It had to be deeper in the room. High in the corners she saw red lights flashing from the motion detectors.

Martika knew she would have to get around the detectors. She calculated the distance and angle of the beams from the flashing lights. If she could shimmy underneath and alongside them, she might avoid triggering the alarm. It was not so different from the work she had been doing in her geometry class with Ms. Loftus. Studying for her final was about to pay off.

She crouched and took her first steps, sliding under the first motion detector beam, afraid to breathe. Nothing. DiCario's voice came over the headset, startling her.

"How's it going in there? Any luck?" he asked.

"I'm in the gallery room, with the artifacts," Martika answered.

"That's great!"

"But the motion detectors are on. I've gotten past one of them but there are two more. I haven't seen the jaguar yet, but I can feel that it's close by."

"Good work. Everything is under control out here." DiCario decided against telling her about the beating he knew Ted must have been getting from the security team.

Martika lay flat against the floor and slithered like a snake toward the back wall of the gallery. The tingling was now pulsing in her head. The whispering had intensified.

I am almost there, Balam. Just a few more feet until I reach you.

She glanced at the flashing red light of the last motion detector, twisted her lower body out of its range and stepped clear of it. She faced a row of statues. No jaguar, but one pedestal stood empty.

"It's not here," she whispered into the headset.

"What?" DiCario's voice shot back.

"There's just an empty pedestal," she explained.

"He must have moved it to another part of the house. Give me a minute to regroup."

Martika walked over to the empty pedestal. The pulsing was strong; she knew the jaguar had been in this spot. She remembered Jennifer's bracelet and Tía Tellín's leather-bound volume. She closed her eyes and reached her hands out, laying them in the center of the pedestal. A succession of images filled her mind.

The narrow stairway . . . the yellow light at the top . . .
the chuffing of the big cat from the darkness below . . .
a weathered, rustic door with an iron bolt.

Her eyes snapped open. It was the scene from her dream. And the door she had just passed in the corridor. She took out the envelope of money and laid it on the empty pedestal.

"Sorry to disturb your collection," she whispered, "but the Jaguar of Uxmal is ready to go home."

On the far side of the house, Buzz walked briskly down the north corridor, stopping to check with the housekeepers who were changing the linens in the master suite.

"You ladies see or hear anything strange in the house? We had a guy outside trying to sneak in."

The main housekeeper shook her head nervously.

"No one has been in here as far as I know."

He gave her a wink and pushed open the door to give a quick glance around the luxurious master bathroom. He moved to the hallway. The north corridor was clear. All he had to do was loop around to the south side of the house. He would be done in a matter of minutes.

"Okay, according the floor plan, there is another room that holds mostly canvases and sculpture on the northwest side of house. You can get there by passing through the family room," DiCario explained as Martika slid past the final motion detector.

"No, it's in a room I passed, on the south corridor," she interrupted him.

"According to the plans we have it has to be—" DiCario insisted.

"No. I know where it is," Martika cut him off, silently pushing through the glass doors and treading down the hallway, retracing her steps.

"Martika, be careful. Listen to what he's saying. He's done this kind of thing before," Lola's voice chimed in.

Ramón agreed, overlapping her. "She's right. You have to listen to DiCario."

"So if you turn right, just as you pass the game room . . ." DiCario's voice cut annoyingly into Martika's thoughts.

"I can't do this with everyone talking at me. I know where it is. I'm getting it and then coming out the way I came in," Martika said.

"No, Martika, you have to follow the floor plan. There are only two rooms that house the artworks . . ." DiCario insisted. Martika pulled off the headset, sticking it into her back pocket.

Trust your instincts. You would not have been called if you were not powerful enough.

The tingling grew stronger as she approached the rustic

wooden door. She lifted the bolt and pulled it open. She was at the top of a steep stairway. On the wall, a light switch. This was the place.

I have arrived, Balam. I am here.

She began her descent into the darkness.

Twenty-One

❀

*T*he security team gave Ted a final shove off the property just as Ilse, the dog trainer, returned with the German shepherds. The dogs lunged instinctively for him and she held them tight, looking away from Ted. R.J. Hayes didn't pay her to ask questions, just to keep the dogs in shape. Whoever the bruised and battered fellow was outside the gate, he was not her business. She set the dogs loose once the gates were closed, and she got into her Range Rover without a backward glance. On the rain gutter, a black crow perched, watching.

On the bluff, Ramón and Lola watched through binoculars with growing panic. The trainer drove away and the guard dogs now patrolled the property. The security team took their original positions.

"We should call the police," Lola said.

Ramón looked at his watch. It had been eighteen minutes since Martika had gone inside.

"She told us to give her thirty minutes," Ramón replied.

"Yes, but that was before she took off the damn headset! How is she going to get out with those dogs outside?"

"Give her another minute. She said she was close. She's got to put the headset back on before she tries to come out," Ramón replied just as Ted appeared around the corner of the rocks. His shirt was torn and his cheek split open. One eye was swollen shut and he held his ribs in pain. He had hoped to find Martika waiting with the others. He didn't need to ask. He could see from their troubled expressions that she was still inside the house.

Buzz walked slowly down the south corridor, checking each room. Something felt wrong. He entered the artifact gallery and leaned down, looking closely at the floor. The housekeepers had just waxed the floors, and in the shiny finish he saw clearly the print of a small tennis shoe. It didn't belong to any of the house staff. R.J. Hayes didn't allow his employees to wear tennis shoes. Someone was in the house after all. The muscles at the back of his neck twitched, and Buzz took the safety off his hand gun. He laid his face low to the floor and saw it plainly: a trail of small footprints. They led out the door and up the corridor. Buzz got up and followed them.

❀　❀　❀

By the time Martika reached the bottom of the staircase, her eyes had adjusted to the darkness. She remembered the details of her dream, how the jaguar had been seated in the stone alcove. There was no alcove, just racks and racks of wine bottles. The wine cellar was cool and smelled of the salt air.

Why would R.J. Hayes put a valuable artifact in a damp room at the bottom of his house? Maybe her instinct was wrong. Maybe she should have listened to DiCario. But the tingling was a steady beat in her head, and the whispering of the voices was almost audible. What were they saying? She closed her eyes and reached out to her ancestors across the dimensions.

Help me, Xusita. Help me, Soraya. Help me find the jaguar. I've come this far. . . .

She heard a faint cracking in the rock wall. A small stream of pebbles fell from a large stone slab behind the door. Martika moved to it quickly, running her fingers over the stone, pushing and prodding. Suddenly it popped open as if on a spring. She pulled the stone away. A deep cavern had been carved into the stone; R.J. Hayes's secret hideaway. She reached in and ran her hands over the stone. Far at the back of the cavern, she felt the jaguar. She grabbed it carefully and pulled it out. A surge of power emanated from it. A hum vibrated through her whole body.

I have found you and I will return you to your home.

Martika heard footsteps at the top of the stairs. The door creaked open. Someone was up there.

On the bluff, Ted checked his watch again. Twenty-two minutes. He reached for Lola's headset and took out his cell phone.

"I'm calling the police, DiCario. There's been no word from her for the last five minutes. I was a fool to try this. We can't let her get hurt."

DiCario's voice came back. "She said she knew where it was, in a room off the south corridor. She sounded certain. Maybe we should give her another minute?"

Ramón was about to speak up when they heard Martika's voice.

"It's me. I'm in the wine cellar."

Ted answered. "Martika, you have to get out of there! It all went wrong. The guards are back in position—the dogs are on the property. Just give up and get out, even if you get caught. I'll take responsibility for the whole thing."

"I'm okay. I—" The line of communication was broken.

"Martika? Are you there?" Ramón asked. No answer.

Martika looked around the stone room. There were no windows. The only way out was up the staircase. She clutched the jaguar statue to her and put her hand out in the darkness. Salty air was seeping in through a vent that led somewhere out of the room. It was her only hope. She hoisted herself on top of several cases of wine and pulled at the grate over the vent. It held fast. She remembered Ramón's Swiss Army knife. Carefully holding the jaguar, she flipped open the knife. She reached high to the corners of the grate and felt for the screws.

At the top of the stairs someone flicked the yellow light on. Martika worked faster, twisting the small metal screws furiously. She had pushed the grate partially aside when she heard his voice.

"Well, what do we have here?" Buzz asked, his hand ready on his gun.

Martika whipped around, almost losing her balance.

"Careful there, little lady—you don't want to break that statue, especially since it doesn't belong to you."

"It doesn't belong to Mr. Hayes, either. I left the money for it back in the gallery, on the pedestal."

"Well, aren't you a good girl?" he said sarcastically, as he inched toward her. Martika backed up against the wall.

"It was on the black market. It was stolen hundreds of years ago from the place where it belongs," she explained nervously.

Now Buzz was just a few feet away from her. "My, you're just a little Indiana Jones, aren't you? And quite a pretty one at that."

Martika looked at his eyes, glaring at her, a cruel smile on his thin lips. Her heart was pounding.

Help me, Balam. I have come here for you. Help me. . . .

Buzz stuck the gun back into his waistband, confident in his own strength. He took a menacing step toward her when Martika felt it, rising up her spine and shooting through her limbs. The jaguar in her arms seemed to glow, and Martika felt it behind her eyes before it flashed out and exploded in the air between them. A ball of flame. Soraya's Fire.

"What the hell?!" Buzz yelled as smoke filled the room and the flames began to spread to the wooden crates. Martika stared at it in shock, not moving. Then she heard the sharp cry of a bird coming from the vent. She pulled away the grate and climbed into the duct.

This is my dream—the tunnel, crawling, the salt air. Keep moving forward . . . don't turn back.

At the far end of the vent duct she saw a black crow watching her from the other side of the metal grate that led to the beach outside. Smoke and flames danced at the open mouth of the vent. She had to keep moving if she didn't want to be overcome by them. She crawled toward the grate, the crow never taking its eyes from her. She could hear the waves breaking against the shore. She kicked at the grate but it held fast. Martika watched in amazement as the crow pecked furiously at the edges of the grate, loosening it from the silty rock. Martika's head was light; she felt as if she might faint at any moment. In the wine cellar the flames began to spark at the mouth of the tunnel, drawn to the stream of fresh air. The crow grabbed the grate in its beak as Martika gave it a final kick and tumbled out, rolling with the jaguar tucked against her body. Flames roared down the vent, shooting out the open end. The crow took flight, leaving the grate lying on the sand. Martika dragged herself up and began running down the beach.

"Okay, it's been long enough! I'm calling the police now!" Ted shouted into the headset at DiCario.

Lola and Ramón scanned the beach and the Hayes property with binoculars.

"Go ahead. It can't be good. Get them out here ASAP," DiCario agreed.

Ted flipped open his phone and dialed 911. The call was on its second ring when Lola suddenly shouted, "I think I see her! She's running this way!"

Ted grabbed the binoculars and looked. In the distance, against the shimmering of the breaking waves, he saw a small form running toward them.

"Hold on everyone, it might be her," he said to DiCario and his team. Ted kept the binoculars trained on the figure. It was Martika, the jaguar statue held tight against her chest, her black hair loose in the wind as she ran stumbling toward the bluff.

Twenty-Two

❀

Ted and the others were waiting at the bottom of the wooden staircase when Martika got there. Exhausted, she collapsed at their feet. They carried her up and put her into the back of Ted's car. Lola climbed in beside her.

"She's barely conscious. We have to take her to a hospital!" she said, terrified.

Martika shook her head and whispered, "Take me to Tía Tellín's. She'll know what to do."

"Where's that?" Ted asked.

"In our neighborhood. Follow me!" Ramón replied, running for the Fiesta.

Ted climbed into his car and gunned the engine, looking back at Martika's prone form. He reached out and squeezed her hand, which was wrapped tightly around the jaguar.

"You did it, Martika. You did the impossible, all on your own."

Martika did not respond. She had fallen into a deep sleep. The Benz drove closely behind the Fiesta with DiCario's Expedition pulling up the rear as the fire engines roared past them down Pacific Coast Highway, to the smoke rising from the R.J. Hayes estate.

Martika lay propped against the pillows on Tía Tellín's claw-foot couch. Lola and Ramón sat beside her.

"*Abre, mija.* Open up," Tía Tellín told her, pouring another shot of strong-smelling tea down Martika's throat. Martika swallowed with difficulty.

"That's disgusting," she said weakly to Tía Tellín.

"Oh good, you're going to survive!" Lola said, relieved. The jaguar sat on the bookcase, its emerald eyes staring at them. Ted talked on his cell phone to Blasi's people.

"Okay, tonight. One A.M, straight up at the first lookout point past Beverly Glen and Mulholland. I'll be there with the statue. You have my daughter—*unharmed*." He hung up and turned to Martika.

"So you got into the wine cellar and then what? How did you get out when Buzz came down after you?"

Martika glanced nervously at her aunt. Tía Tellín never took her amber eyes off Martika, who explained, "I climbed through the grate before he could reach me."

Tía Tellín raised a questioning eyebrow. She turned over Martika's hand and saw that her palms were red and blistered. Martika looked away, knowing her aunt had figured out the truth about Soraya's Fire. They would have that discussion in private.

"So what are you going to tell your mom? She must wonder where you've been all day," Lola asked.

"I told her we were going to the downtown library, to study for finals. You'll back me up?"

Ramón and Lola nodded in agreement.

"And the jaguar?" Martika looked at Tía Tellín. To her surprise, Tía Tellín picked up the statue and handed it to Ted.

"This is yours, Mr. Colton. Good luck getting your daughter back safely."

"Thank you for everything," he said, and turned to Martika. "And without you, I would never have been able to do it at all. Everything went wrong, but you came through. Thank you. All of you."

Martika's mind was racing. How could Tía Tellín let him walk away with the jaguar statue? After everything they had gone through to get it back?

Ted wrapped the statue in a soft cotton cloth that Tía Tellín had given him, and left.

Before she could ask her question, Tía Tellín put a hand

on Martika's shoulder.

"Don't worry. The Balam made it safe thus far. He will be back before dawn."

Mojito checked the bullets in his Saturday night special. A full load. One or two well placed shots fired into the night on a deserted stretch of highway, and he'd get rid of Jennifer's father once and for all. He'd head straight down south with the girl for the reward he so richly deserved. Blasi wouldn't mind once he got over that business of the statue.

It was payoff night and Mojito was looking forward to it. He smoked another crank-laced cigarette, getting himself primed for the evening. He pulled up to the abandoned building where Jennifer was waiting. Showtime.

Jennifer sat in the backseat, her hands tied, while Mojito sang along with a song from an oldies radio station.

"Without you, I was nothing, baby . . . Without you, I was all alone . . . Didn't have someone to hold me . . . No love to call my own." He dissolved into laughter at the end of the song. He looked at Jennifer in the rearview mirror.

"You know that old song, *güera*? It's way before your time and mine. But it's cool—the *veteranos* listen to it." He hummed the melody as the car wound its way through the city.

The quiet streets of downtown gave way to the busy nightlife of Hollywood. They drove past the Cinerama Dome and turned onto the Cahuenga Corridor, passing Beauty Bar and White Lotus, with limousines lined up outside and black-suited doormen manning the velvet rope. The car rumbled up to Mulholland Highway, where the street became deserted except for the odd set of high beams coming toward them and then disappearing around the next turn.

They passed the big gated homes perched at the end of long driveways and Jennifer thought of the people inside, oblivious to what was happening outside their doors.

Even if I screamed, no one would hear me. If I ran, no one would know I was out here.

Jennifer knew something was up. Mojito's mood was too happy for him to be returning her to her father. "Where are we meeting my dad?" she asked.

"You'll see. You ever been across the border, *güera?* Down into Tijuana?"

"Once, a long time ago," she answered.

Mojito chuckled to himself. "You'd like it." He turned up the volume on the radio as the lights of the San Fernando Valley came into view, stretching out for miles.

At the lookout point, Ted sat in his car, smoking a cigarette. Any minute now Blasi's people would be arriving with Jennifer. He ran his hand over the jaguar in the seat beside him. He'd learned his lesson this time. No more black market transactions, no more dealing with lowlifes like Blasi and

Hayes. *I'll make an honest living selling cars,* he resolved wryly.

He heard the rumbling of Mojito's car approaching before he saw it. The Mustang pulled up to the lookout point. Ted couldn't see anything through the tinted windows. Mojito took his time getting out.

"You Blasi's guy?" Ted asked, emerging from his car.

"That's right," Mojito answered, his face expressionless.

"Where's my daughter?"

"You have what Mr. Blasi wants?"

"Right here."

Jennifer watched through the window as her father held out the jaguar statue. Mojito took it and set it on the hood of the car. He reached for the gun hidden in his waistband. She saw it and shouted, "Daddy, watch out!! He has a gun!"

Ted heard her voice but he couldn't make out what she was saying.

"Where's Jennifer?" He took a step toward the car, but Mojito stopped him with the snub nosed barrel of the gun. Jennifer tried to open the car door with her bound hands, but Mojito had activated the child security locks. All she could do was bang on the window with her fists and watch.

"What's wrong with her?" Ted asked anxiously. "Let her out! We made the trade!"

Mojito smiled at him maliciously. "You think I'm gonna let you take my pretty little *güera* from me? Now that I've gotten so used to her? As far as Blasi's going to know, you tried to stiff him. You should have brought some backup with you, man. You're making my job too easy." With his finger on the trigger he backed Ted toward a steep ravine.

"There's so many coyotes up here, they'll probably find bits and pieces of you," Mojito said, enjoying himself. Jennifer looked away, unable to watch what was about to happen.

"Adios, papacito," Mojito said, raising the gun just as a team of police charged out of the surrounding bushes. Several unmarked police cars arrived, cutting off the road access.

"Police! Don't move! Drop your weapon!" a ninja-suited policeman shouted at Mojito.

"DROP IT!" The cop advanced, his weapon trained on Mojito's forehead.

Mojito dropped the gun to his side as several cops moved in on him and cuffed his hands behind his back. A detective jimmied the car door open, and Ted pulled Jennifer from the backseat, embracing her.

"You're safe now, honey. Daddy's here."

She wrapped her arms around his neck and buried her face in his shoulder. The detective stepped forward and introduced himself.

"Mr. Colton, I'm Detective John Guest."

Ted pumped his hand vigorously. "How did you know we would be here? I never called the police—Blasi warned me not to. I just finalized the plans this afternoon."

Detective Guest smiled at him and answered, "We have a confidential source."

Jennifer saw Mojito glaring at her as he was pushed into the back of a police car. Curious residents peered out from the big houses. Jennifer put her arm around her father and asked, "What happened to your face? You're all messed up."

Ted smiled. "It's a long story. . . ."

Twenty-Three

❀

It was almost two o'clock in the morning when Detective Guest arrived at Tía Tellín's house. There was a single light on in the window. He tapped on the door. Tía Tellín opened it and motioned him inside.

"Detective Guest, to what do I owe the pleasure of this late-night call?"

With a smile he handed her the brown bag he had been carrying. Tía Tellín reached in and pulled out the statue of the jaguar.

"We had a bust out on Mulholland, a kidnapping ransom drop. Luckily we caught the perpetrator and everything worked out. But this seems to have been left behind somehow. You know how it is with police work. Sometimes evidence gets lost. I thought you might know who it belongs to?" he asked.

Tía Tellín took his hand.

"Thank you, John," she said.

"No, thank you for the tip on the ransom drop. Once I had specifics, the lieutenant was willing to give me some backup. Putting a tail on Colton was easy. And when you filled us in on the time and place, it was just a matter of waiting. Good thing, too. That Mojito character was ready to knock off Colton and take the girl down to Mexico. Now we can finally get something on Eddie Blasi."

They walked toward the door. Guest was unable to hide his curiosity and asked, "I just want to know how you figured out the location of the drop? Did you have a vision or something? A premonition?"

Tía Tellín said dryly, "Nothing that magical, I'm afraid. I heard Ted Colton making the arrangements right here on the phone in my living room."

Detective Guest laughed. He turned to leave. "Same time on Thursday? At the corner of the park?"

"I have to make a trip out of town this week," she replied.

"Then I'll see you next week. Lock the door, now." He got into his car and drove away. Tía Tellín stood on the porch for a long time, looking at the jaguar in the moonlight.

Ya es hora, Balam. The time has come.

"Listen to this! They found Jennifer!" Aurelia turned up the local television news station as she added the scrambled eggs to a skillet of sizzling *chorizo*. Martika came out from her bedroom, her eyes red from exhaustion. The well-coiffed newscaster on the television was saying, "The teenage daughter of luxury car dealer Ted Colton of Colton Motors had been held for over a week in an abandoned building in the industrial section of downtown Los Angeles. The girl was unharmed but relieved to be reunited with her family. . . ."

Aurelia smiled at Martika. "I knew it would work out. He may live on the edge, but Mr. Colton is *buena gente*. I have to call and congratulate him! Imagine how relieved the mother must be!"

Martika nodded and poured herself a glass of juice. "That's amazing. I'm glad she's okay," she said.

Aurelia looked at Martika closely. "I think you spent too much time in the library yesterday, *mija*. Your eyes are all red. You need to take a break from studying today, *entiendes*?"

Martika suppressed a smile. "Sure, Mom. Whatever you say."

Aurelia spooned a steaming pile of spicy *chorizo con huevos* onto Martika's plate.

"You know, your papi is supposed to have his visit with you this afternoon, and he thought he'd take that old hibachi out to the park and make some *carne asada*. What do you think?"

"Yeah! Can we invite Lola and Ramón?"

"Of course, invite the whole family," Aurelia said.

Martika hugged her mother around the waist. "And Tía Tellín?"

Aurelia smiled at her as she placed the hot tortillas into a warming basket. "*Claro que si, mija*. She's your aunt, after all."

When Martika pushed open the gate to Tía Tellín's yard, she was surprised to see a driver putting a suitcase into the trunk of his cab. Tía Tellín stepped out of the house wearing a traveling suit and a hat perched on her head. She carried an old-fashioned carpet bag.

"Are you going somewhere, Tía?"

"I'll be back in a few days, a week at the most. You and I have to talk about what happened in that wine cellar, Martika," Tía Tellín said seriously.

"There's something I want to ask *you*, Tía. There was a black crow waiting for me outside the vent duct. It picked at the grate and helped me get out."

"Really? Animals can be so smart sometimes," Tía Tellín replied, buttoning her gloves.

"Was that you, Tía? I know that *curanderas* can shape-shift."

Tía Tellín just smiled mysteriously and said, "I believe we were talking about *you* and Soraya's Fire. What happened in there?"

"I didn't do it on purpose, I swear. It just came out of me. I asked the Balam for help and it just . . . happened," Martika explained.

Tía Tellín took her hand and looked at the palm.

"I see the blisters have disappeared. You were lucky this time, Martika. You survived and you completed your task. But when I return I will tell you the whole story of Soraya's Fire. That will be part of your training, making sure that you learn how to control this gift in the future. You can't have spontaneous bursts of fire coming out of you when you get worked up."

"I understand, Tía."

"After all, you're fifteen now. Imagine what could happen if that handsome Ramón Lopez kissed you? You might burn the house down," Tía Tellín said with a sly grin.

Martika blushed. "Ramón? He's like my brother!"

As the cab driver held open the door, Tía Tellín leaned in and whispered, "Yes, but he's not your brother, is he? We *curanderas* can see a lot of things, *mija*."

"Whatever!" Martika said, giving her a playful push into the backseat of the cab. It was backing away when Martika shouted, "Tía! I forgot! What happened to the jaguar? Did you get it back?"

Tía Tellín took it from the carpetbag and held it up through the open window for her to see.

"I told you it would all work out the way it was supposed to, Martika. The Balam came back before dawn. *Cuídate!*"

The cab disappeared down the hill. Martika watched it go, wondering how Tía Tellín had gotten the jaguar back. She remembered her aunt's words that first day. *You can use your powers to do good.* And she had. Jennifer and the jaguar were safe. She began walking down the steep hill toward home. The purple flowers of the jacaranda trees fell, tickling the back of her neck.

Aurelia was packing up a basket of food for the cookout. Camiso climbed a ladder, searching for the hibachi in the hall closet.

"Careful, *viejo*, you're going to fall and break your neck!" Aurelia shouted at him as she loaded the fresh jicama and *chile con limón* into a plastic container. The doorbell rang.

"Martika! Get the door. I'm up to my elbows in *nopales*!" Aurelia said.

Martika opened the door. Ted, Nancy, and Jennifer stood in the hallway.

"Hi!" she said, surprised. Aurelia came out from the kitchen and shrieked when she saw Jennifer.

"I knew you'd come back safe, *mija*. I just knew it! Didn't I tell you, Martika?" she said, throwing her arms around Jennifer.

"Well, I thought it was only right to come by and see you, after all—" Ted stopped mid-sentence when he saw Martika shaking her head and putting her finger to her lips behind her mother's back. Aurelia looked at him expectantly and he went on, "After all, we got your call this morning. It was very considerate of you," he covered.

"Well, of course I was going to call when I saw the news!! Come in, come in." She ushered them into the apartment.

Camiso emerged, triumphant, with the hibachi.

"I got it, *vieja*! It was way in the back but I got it!" Aurelia looked at Ted and his ex-wife, unsure how to introduce Camiso.

"This is my dad." Martika spoke up.

"We're just getting ready to go have a barbecue in the park. Would you like to join us?" Aurelia asked.

"Oh no, we don't want to be any bother," Ted said.

Aurelia waved away his concern. "It's no bother. And it's a day to celebrate your daughter's return!"

"I'd love to," said Nancy. "I never barbecue in New York."

"Excellent! Martika, you and Jennifer go get the blanket from the linen closet. We don't want grass stains on our clothes," Aurelia said with authority.

Once they were out of earshot, Jennifer turned to Matika and said, "My dad told me everything you did. About the dreams and the pool house. And going into the Hayes estate alone for the statue. It was really intense."

"Yeah, I guess it was," Martika replied.

"I have something for you." Jennifer pulled the gold charm bracelet with the animal figures from her pocket. She tried to hand it to Martika, who shook her head.

"I can't take that. It's from your grandma," Martika said.

"I want you to have it. It's what brought you into this whole thing. If it hadn't been for you, I don't want to think about where I'd be."

Martika took the delicate bracelet and put it on her wrist. "Thank you," she said.

"No, thank *you*," Jennifer corrected her.

From the kitchen Aurelia shouted, "Come on, girls! I've got Mr. Colton loaded up like a *burro!*"

As they walked back up the hallway, Jennifer asked suddenly, "What are you doing next week?"

"I have finals," Martika said.

"Me too."

"And I'm not ready for them."

"Me either. I was thinking, do you want to go to the beach on Saturday? We could bring our books and study. And we could go swimming."

"And study," said Martika.

"And sleep," said Jennifer.

"And *study!*" they said together, laughing.

"I don't know, it takes a long time to get there on the bus," Martika said.

"I'll come and pick you up. That's what that crazy convertible is for, isn't it? To drive around with the top down with your friends?" Jennifer asked.

Martika smiled at the idea. Then she added, "Great. But we have to take Lola. She's already jealous of you. She'll be impossible if she can't come."

"My dad told me she was like James Bond, with the binoculars out on the bluff," Jennifer said, impressed.

Martika laughed. "Yeah, James Bond with hair products and lip gloss!"

"Ready?" Aurelia asked. She gave Ted a pile of CDs and Nancy a boom box to carry.

"*Lista, Mami,*" said Martika.

"*¡Ya vámonos!*" Aurelia called out as they walked the narrow stairway to the street.

Out in Echo Park, several paddleboats worked their way across the water, their colorful canopies flapping in the breeze. The Sunday traffic on the freeway was slow and steady, a fraction of the usual gridlock. Camiso tossed several thin pieces of *carne asada* onto the grill. José, Lola's father, cast approving glances at the preparation. Ted was opening his second Corona when Lola popped a Carlos Vives CD into the boom box and grabbed him by the hand.

"Mr. Colton, do you know how to cumbia?" she asked. Ted shook his head.

"Well, you're going to learn now! She's the cumbia queen!" Ramón added as "Volver al Valle" began to play. He smiled at Martika until she looked away, embarrassed at the memory of Tía Tellín's parting words.

Aurelia and Patricia, Lola's mother, explained to Nancy how to make *nopalito* salad by marinating the cactus in lime juice and *pico de gallo*. They didn't notice when Javier wandered over.

"Hey, Mom. You guys having a party?" he asked.

Patricia put her arm around his shoulder and whispered, "Where've you been all day, *mijo*? Let me introduce you."

She led him to where Lola and Ted were dancing.

"Mr. Colton, Jennifer, this is my younger son, Javier," she said.

Javier froze when he saw Jennifer. The *veteranos* had been talking about how Mojito was picked up by the police for taking part in *la güera's* kidnapping. Javier had been lying low all day, terrified that they'd be looking for him next. Now, face-to-face with Jennifer, he knew she would turn him in. His impulse was to run. Before he could move, Jennifer walked up to him with her hand outstretched.

"Jennifer Colton," she said. "Nice to meet you."

Tía Tellín got off the Aeroméxico flight in Cancún and walked past the porters trying to entice travelers to the newest beach resorts and hotels. The sun was beginning to set when she boarded a bus headed for the interior of the Yucatán peninsula, far from the discos and party atmosphere of Cancún. She rode late into the night, passing through one small, remote town after another. The women on the dusty streets wore traditional dress, their strong Indian features revealing an almost undiluted Mayan bloodline.

The bus traveled into the jungle, where the air became thick and tropical. It stopped at a fork in the road marked only by a large ceiba tree. Carrying her suitcase and the carpetbag, Tía Tellín climbed down from the bus, past the other passengers with caged chickens and colorful baskets filled with fruits and vegetables. She stepped into the dark night. The moon was hidden behind the dense clouds. She strode down a dirt path that led into the jungle. Soon she was swallowed up in the lush greenery.

Tía Tellín's shoes were muddy when she finally arrived at a small hut. She was about to knock on the door when a tiny, wizened Indian woman opened it. She had been waiting. She gestured for Tía Tellín to come inside and offered her a cup of steaming tea. Without speaking, Tía Tellín took the jaguar statue from the carpetbag and handed it to the old woman, who ran her hands over its features. Then she fixed her cloudy, amber eyes on Tía Tellín and asked, "*¿Cómo lo encontraste? ¿Después de tantos años?*" How did you find it after all these years?

"*No fui yo, aunque yo quisiera decirte que sí.*" It wasn't me, although I'd like to say it was.

"*¿Quién fue?*" Who was it?

"*La nueva, la próxima en nuestra linea.*" The new one, the next in our line.

"*¿Donde está? No la he visto aquí en la selva ni en mis sueños.*" Where is she? I haven't seen her here in the jungle, nor in my dreams.

"*Es una muchacha del mundo moderno, vive lejos . . . pero es poderosa, inocente, y llena de esperanza.*" She is a girl from the modern world. She lives far away but she is powerful, innocent, and full of hope.

"*Pues la esperanza es la cosa mas poderosa en la vida. ¿Cómo se ve?*" Well, hope is the most powerful thing in the world. What does she look like?

"*Se ve como todas nosotras, piel canela, pelo negro y los ojos de gato.*" She looks like all of us, brown skin, black hair, eyes like a cat.

The old woman smiled and nodded her head.

"*¿Y cómo se llama?*" And what is her name?

"*Se llama Martika Gálvez.*" Her name is Martika Gálvez.

Spanish Words and Phrases

abuela • grandmother

agua de sandía • watermelon juice

"Ay, mariposa de amor, mi mariposa de amor. Ya no regreso contigo . . ." • "Ah, butterfly of love, my butterfly of love, I will not come back to you . . ." From the popular song "Mariposa Traicionera," a hit recording by Maná.

Bacabs • Mayan deities who hold up the four corners of the world

Balam-Agab • one of the names for the Mayan jaguar god of the night

bruja • witch

bubalek • a type of traditional drum

buena gente • good people or good person

Bueno, me voy. • Well, I'm going.

burro • donkey

café con leche • coffee mixed with milk

¡Cállate, mujer! • Shut up, woman!

carne asada • traditional Mexican dish of thin beefsteak, cooked on a grill

carnicería • Mexican meat market

carnitas • roasted pork, chopped up

cenote • a large, natural well specific to the Yucatán peninsula. Believed by the Mayans to be the gateway to the land of the dead.

chachalaca • chatterbox, a type of bird

chaskas • traditional rattles made from bone and shells

chile con limón • a sprinkling of dried chile with a dash of lemon, usually put on fresh fruit

chile verde • traditional Mexican dish of pork cooked with green chiles

chorizo • Mexican sausage, often prepared with scrambled eggs

chorizo con huevos • sausage with eggs

claro que sí • of course

cojones • testicles, balls. To have cojones is to have guts.

Corazón Sagrado • image of the Sacred Heart. Jesus points to his heart, which is encircled by a crown of thorns.

Corazón Salvaje • *Wild Heart* or *Savage Heart*, a famous telenovela on Spanish-language television

crudo • hangover

¡Cuídate! • Take care of yourself!

cumbia • a traditional style of music and a popular dance

curandera • traditional healer, medicine woman. The *curandera* is often considered akin to a witch or wizard, with psychic powers of divination and astral projection.

¡Dime! • Tell me!

Dime, mi amor, ¿crees que tu esposo anda con otra? • Tell me, my dear, do you think your husband is seeing another woman?

Dios mio • my God

¿Entendiste? • Do you understand?

esa • that

excelente • excellent

futbolistas • soccer players

gabacho • white or Caucasian

gente • people

guayabera • shirt with embroidery detail, traditional throughout Latin America

güera • fair: blond-haired, light-skinned

güerita • diminutive of *güera*; little fair one. (See also *-ito/-ita*.)

¡Hasta el domingo! • See you Sunday!

hola • hello

Hola, mija. ¿Que haces aqui tan temprano? ¿Todo esta bien con tu mama? • Hello, my dear. What are you doing here so early? Is everything all right with your mother?

hombre • man

huipil • traditional embroidered dress worn by Mayan women

incensario • traditional incense holder

indio • Indian

-ito/-ita • diminutive, familiar of a noun

Itzamná • Supreme deity of the Maya

Ixchel • moon goddess, supreme female deity of the Maya

jefe • chief, boss

Kinich Ahau • the sun god of the Maya

kuyum • a type of traditional drum

la Mona esa • that Mona, a play on words: *mona* also means female monkey.

la nena • familiar way of referring to a daughter or young girl

linda • pretty

lista • ready

mercado • market

mi princesa • my princess

mijo/mija • slang abbreviation of *mi hijo* (my son) or *mi hija* (my daughter)

mujer desenfrenada • wild woman, literally "woman without brakes"

mujersota • Mexican slang term for a voluptuous, well-built girl

nagual/naguala • sorcerer, magician, wizard, shape-shifter

niña mimada • spoiled girl

¡No me mientes! • Don't lie to me!

¡No seas grosero! • Don't be rude [or vulgar]!

No te preocupes. • Don't worry.

nopalito • cactus, usually sliced and marinated

Norteña music • regional style of music popular in areas along the U.S.-Mexico border

pan blanco • white bread

papacito • affectionate term for one's boyfriend, husband, or child. Mojito's use of it with Ted is a taunt to Ted's powerlessness in that situation.

Parece indio. • It looks Indian.

pendejo • derogatory term for jerk

Pero ya ha llegado la hora . . . pasen, están en su casa. • But now the time has come. Come in, you are in your home. (Final phrase is a familiar Mexican greeting and invitation into someone's home.)

picadillo • hash; minced-up meat

pico de gallo • fresh salsa made of chopped chiles, tomato, and onion

pinche maquillaje • *pinche* is a derogatory, slang word, popular in Mexico; *maquillaje* is makeup

pollita • little chicken; slang term for a young woman

por Dios • by God

Pues creo que sí porque no regresó anoche hasta las tres de la mañana. • Well, I think so because he didn't come home last night until three in the morning.

¡Qué chingada! • What the f____!

¿Qué haces aquí, viejo? Adelante. • What are you doing here, old man? Come inside. (See also *viejo/vieja*.)

¡Qué machote! • What a big macho!

¡Qué milagro! • What a miracle!

quebradita • a contemporary style of dance

quesadilla • a folded tortilla with melted cheese inside

quinceañera • traditional birthday celebration for a girl of fifteen, comparable to a sweet sixteen party

sangre de gallína • chicken blood

santitos • "little saints"; saints' images

"Solamente Una Vez" • "Only Once," or "Only One Time," a famous romantic bolero by Mexican composer Agustín Lara

sopa de fideos • Mexican soup made with vermicelli

suelta la lengua, chica • start talking, girl

teponaxtli • a type of traditional drum

Tía Tellín • Aunt Tellín. *Tellín* is the nickname for *Eleuteria*. It is pronounced "Teh-yin."

¡Tu tienes la culpa! • You are to blame!

tunkul • a type of traditional drum

velorio • wake for a deceased person

¡venga! • come here!

veteranos • veterans; a street term used to refer to long-time gang members

viejo/vieja: • old man/old woman; slang term used commonly among Mexicans to refer to a spouse

"Volver al Valle" • "Return to the Valley," a popular song by Carlos Vives

Xibalba • the Mayan underworld

ya basta • enough already

ya es hora • it's time

¡Ya vámonos! • Let's go!

yerbabuena • spearmint

zacatán • a type of traditional drum